ALSO BY

MASSIMO CARLOTTO

The Goodbye Kiss
Death's Dark Abyss
The Fugitive
Poisonville (with Marco Videtta)
Bandit Love

AT THE END OF A DULL DAY

Massimo Carlotto

AT THE END OF A DULL DAY

Translated from the Italian
by Antony Shugaar

Europa Editions
214 West 29th Street
New York, N.Y. 10001
www.europaeditions.com
info@europaeditions.com

First Publication 2013 by Europa Editions

Translation by Antony Shugaar
Original title: *Alla fine di un giorno noioso*

Library of Congress Cataloging in Publication Data is available
ISBN 978-1-60945-114-1

Carlotto, Massimo
At the End of a Dull Day

Book design by Emanuele Ragnisco
www.mekkanografici.com

Cover illustration by Igort

Prepress by Grafica Punto Print – Rome

Printed in the USA

Ruby Heartstealer taught us one more time:
Screwing the powerful is never a crime
(Graffiti in blue paint on a wall in Padua)

CONTENTS

AT THE END
OF A DULL DAY

CHAPTER ONE
At the End of a Dull Day

At the end of a dull day, the lawyer and, incidentally, parliamentarian of the Italian republic, Sante Brianese strode with his customary briskness into La Nena. A moment later his secretary and his personal assistant appeared in the doorway. Ylenia and Nicola. Good-looking, well dressed, young, and cheerful. They looked like something straight out of an American TV show.

It was aperitif time in the establishment, and there was a steady flow of customers, drinks, and hors d'oeuvres. Outside on the patio, mushroom-shaped heat lamps kept the tightly packed crowd of smokers warm. I knew almost everybody there. I'd cultivated my clientele over the years with painstaking diligence. There were no cocaine, whores, or dickheads in my bar, and I had a guy on salary who had fried his brains on steroids but who still could be relied upon to stand discreetly outside the door and keep away vendors peddling flowers, cigarette lighters, and bric-a-brac of all kinds. You could only get into La Nena if you were looking to pay reasonable prices in exchange for a peaceful, refined, and yet "bubbly and amusing" atmosphere. Mornings, from 8 to 10, we served fine teas, fragrant croissants, and cappuccinos made with milk shipped directly to us from a small mountain village in the Dolomites. At noon sharp, the aperitif hour began. From 12:30 to 3 o'clock, we served lunch: a light, high-energy meal for officeworkers and busy professionals, a minimalist vegetarian repast for the overweight on perennial diets, or else a lavish banquet, in the strictest Venetian tradition, for salesmen and clients not worried about their weight. The evening aperitif began at 6:45 and dinner was served from 7:30 on. For ordinary mortals, the kitchen shut down at 10:30. For people like Brianese the restaurant was always open.

The Counselor took a seat at his usual table and his favorite waitress hurried over with the usual glass of fine prosecco that I'd been serving him free of charge for the past eleven years. Then, as usual, the customers lined up to pay their customary respects to their elected representative. Not all of the customers. There was a time when the ritual would have included every single customer in my establishment, but in the upcoming regional elections his party was facing a serious challenge from the Padanos, as they were affectionately dubbed even by their allies. More than a few of my clients were discreetly announcing their shift in allegiance to new masters. Brianese, with the usual smile stamped on his face, accepted the avowals of loyalty and kept a mental checklist of the defectors. Toward the end, it was my turn. I poured myself a glass of prosecco, walked around from behind the bar, and took a seat by his side.

"Things still tough down in Rome?" I asked.

He shrugged. "No worse than usual. The real challenges are up here now," he replied, watching his aides mix with the crowd. With a toolkit of wisecracks and gossip they were doing their best to herd the stragglers back into the fold. They knew their job and they were good at it, but victory was by no means assured. Only on election day would it be possible to reckon the exact percentage of the defeat and the collateral damage in terms of business. Then he turned to look me right in the eye and said: "We need to talk."

"Name a time, Counselor."

"Not now, I'm expecting guests. There'll be four of us, and we'll need the back room."

It was the most exclusive part of La Nena, entirely at the service of Brianese and the business consortiums and cabals that he controlled. I jutted my chin in Ylenia and Nicola's direction. Brianese shook his head. "No, they'll be going home. I have an appointment with three developers."

"Should I tell Nicoletta to come?"

"I feel sure that the gentlemen would appreciate the gesture."

I circled back behind the bar and pulled open a drawer. In it was the cell phone that I use only when I'm calling her.

Nicoletta Rizzardi was an old friend. She was one of the first people I met when I first moved to the Veneto. We'd even been lovers, for a short while. A tall, slender drink of water with a nice big pair of milky white boobs. She'd been divorced for years and was a die-hard smoker. She loved flashy expensive scarves which she wore constantly and with considerable flair. She had worked in the sector of high-end fashion—strictly counterfeits. Then came the wave of competition in that field from African immigrant street vendors, selling the same articles as she was but at half the price. She was forced to move into a new field and settle for a position repping mid-market intimate apparel. Her income dropped accordingly and she'd been scraping by until I approached her with a proposal to go into business with me in a certain endeavor that quickly proved to be a brilliant opportunity and a steady source of income for both of us.

One night when I was talking with Brianese I'd had the brainstorm. The Counselor was complaining about the fact that in this country public figures no longer enjoyed freedom or any right to privacy. Gossip had become the Italian national sport and no politician could afford the risk anymore of having a little fun on the side because of the danger of winding up as fodder for the press. An innocent dalliance could easily turn into the epitaph of a career. Maybe not in Lombardy or Rome, where members of parliament caught dabbling in extramarital sex or snorting lines of cocaine were exonerated by their fellow politicos as "victims of the pressure cooker life they led, unwillingly separated from their families." Here in the Veneto, however, there was just one simple rule: "Do whatever you want, but don't get caught or it's curtains." The real problem came with the call girls themselves. They had become an integral part of the way business was conducted but they constantly proved to be deeply unreliable. These days no one dreamed of obtaining a contract of any size, even for a miserable traffic circle, without kicking in a percentage in kind. Corruption had evolved and those who were willing to settle for cash payments were considered two-bit operators. Now even wives and offspring were eager to grab a little something for themselves when possible: new wallpaper for the house or a Japanese sports car. Everybody seemed to want an extra piece of baksheesh, a gift to console themselves over the fact that they'd become corrupt. But the call girls had become ground zero for investigating magistrates and investigative journalists, and they were such birdbrains that they seemed incapable of keeping their mouths shut. No matter how bad things got, the call girls were always willing to appear on a talk show to make matters worse.

Brianese was right, several times over. I'd worked for a while in a lap dance club and I know a thing or two about the mindset you find in girls who are willing to accept that transaction.

So I took advantage of my experience and put together a small but extremely reliable network of prostitutes under the guise of an escort service. I went to work for Brianese and his friends.

Never more than four girls at a time, exclusively foreigners who knew nobody and were completely ignorant about the city, and we replaced them after exactly six months. Venezuelans, Argentines, and Brazilians with European features, preferably of Italian descent, the offspring of emigrants. And always one Chinese girl for that exotic touch.

The hard part about the Chinese girl was finding one who was even halfway presentable. I had a contact in Prato but he had nothing to show me but girls they were sending to work out of apartments. The problem was this: the Chinese girls assigned as sex workers were precisely those who couldn't keep pace with production in the sweatshops, the ones who could no longer earn their keep. In other words, all I had to choose from was an array of twenty-two-year-old girls with chapped, callused hands who were so beaten down it would have taken a couple of months of rest and relaxation to get them into any kind of shape to spread their legs with at least a hint of a smile on their lips. I always found myself struggling to imagine them nicely made-up, their hair done properly by a professional hairdresser, and decently dressed. In other words, it was a thankless task, but these days you couldn't hope to operate a first-class escort service without at least one Chinese girl. They helped to put the most demanding clients at their ease and they were perfect for clients who had a hard time expressing their desires. Nicoletta described the Chinese girls as "the dolls that Italian males grew up wishing they could play with." That was true only in part. Actually, they were just sex slaves with long practice at satisfying their masters' wishes. Now, my South American girls I got from Mikhail, a Russian in his forties who was as big, strong, and cunning as the Devil himself. Mikhail worked as a gofer and fixer for a prostitution ring run by two former hookers from Naples, in cahoots with one of the most powerful cops in town, who offered them protection. Mikhail let me pick my girls out of a catalogue and, when he was planning the international arrivals, he would just add mine to the list and keep the money for himself. Mikhail warned me against Russian prostitutes. He could of course get me all the Russian girls I wanted. In his homeland prostitution was a thriving institution, completely out of control. Leaving professional prostitutes aside, there was an army of Russian women of all ages willing to trade sexual favors for minor privileges, especially in the workplace. But once they were incorporated into my network, they'd start looking around for clients of their own and become rivals or else they'd find a man willing to keep them.

"Stick to South American girls," he'd told me. "They're less work. As I'm sure you know, the most important thing about whores is to pick them carefully because they can be a tremendous pain in the ass."

I liked the Russian guy; he was cautious and fair-minded. We regularly met in a large highway service plaza not far outside of Bologna. Lots of people coming and going at all hours. I'd park in an area that wasn't monitored by closed-circuit cameras, he'd slip into the car with his laptop under his arm, and he'd start an extended monologue about his name. I'd always assumed it wasn't his real name.

He claimed his full name was Mikhail Aleksandrovich Sholokhov, like the Russian author who won the Nobel Prize for Literature in 1965.

"Why would the Swedes give the prize to a Communist?" he'd ask me each time with exaggerated indignation. "I can understand a dissident, but what's the idea of giving the award to a man who was named a Hero of the Soviet Union not once but twice?"

"No one even remembers his name," I replied.

"It's a good thing. I'd be embarrassed if anyone ever noticed that I have the same name as that guy. You know that I went into a bookshop once and asked for his best-known book, *And Quiet Flows the Don*?"

"It must be out of print," I said, starting to sound like a broken record.

"Which is lucky, too. Do you think they'll reprint it?"

"No way. Who cares about a writer from the Soviet era? Now Putin's in charge, and he happens to be a close friend of our current prime minister."

"Who ought to learn from Putin how to eliminate the danger of scandals," he shot back. "'Eliminate' . . . I don't know if you catch the pun . . . "

He laughed long and loud. At last, he turned on his laptop so he could show me the catalogue.

"All right, now let's talk about women and money, the only two good things about our lives."

I always played along. I knew Mikhail put on that routine so he'd have time to see if there were any detectives lurking in the shadows.

On his laptop, there were nude photographs of each girl in six different poses, so that their best and worst features were clearly evident. The ones who came to work for us were lucky. We sent them to live in comfortable spacious homes, where Nicoletta took personal charge of them. She taught them everything they needed to know about clothing, makeup, perfume, and etiquette. When they weren't busy with paying clients, Nicoletta gave them work modeling her line of intimate apparel, which served as excellent cover. It was also a good way to make them feel special and to ward off the boredom that could quickly turn into depression. Depression could fill their heads with ideas that were bad for business. To date, in fact, none of the girls had caused trouble and I had never had cause to use my fists on any of them. When my partner and I welcomed each new group we made sure that they couldn't miss a shiny pair of brass knuckles apparently left out in plain view on a coffee table—by accident. Even rank beginners knew that brass knuckles were a whore's worst enemy.

Our girls weren't cheap. Whether it was for five minutes or the whole night, the price never changed: two hundred fifty euros; out of that fee, two hundred euros, no less, went directly into the girl's pockets. Despite the high price, none of our customers had ever complained. They were happy to pay extra for a guarantee of discretion. Anyway the money never came out of the customer's wallet. It was always part of the cost of doing business.

The security rules were ironclad. No drugs, just champagne. Cell phones to be left in the car so that some imbecile couldn't take pictures or compromising videos. The encounters took place in various detached villas, scattered throughout the various provinces and rented for short periods through a real estate agency where Nicoletta's brother worked. Only rarely in hotels. When the girls weren't busy entertaining politicians and friends of politicians, they were made available to prosperous foreign industrialists. The company rule was this: only one client a day, but seven days a week.

The girls fooled themselves into believing they'd become princesses until the morning I loaded them into my car, pretending I was taking them to an orgy outside of town and, once I got them to Genoa, selling them to a group of Maltese gangsters for twice what I'd paid for them. I never asked what would happen to them. All I knew was that a few hours later they were already on board a freighter heading for the Maghreb region of northwest Africa or to Spain. That was all that mattered to me.

The minute the girls got out of the car and found themselves surrounded by those ugly mugs in the filthy warehouse that served as the gang's headquarters, they immediately understood the cruel trap they'd been lured into and they began to weep and wail. It was a heartbreaking spectacle, but it only amused the buyers. They laughed heartily as they reached out rough, dirty hands to grab and grope, savoring the impending rape. For that matter, they were old-school gangsters, firmly convinced that if a whore got a taste of hell, then she'd mistake the clients for heavenly angels. At that juncture, I'd point out that they were taking delivery of delicate, valuable merchandise, count my money in a hurry, and hop in my car and head home.

Every time, the Maltese gangsters asked me to point out the finest of the group, the one that they assumed had spent the most time in my bed. I'd point to one at random, because the last thing I would dream of doing was fuck any of them. After all, I was the boss, and picking one in particular would have just created bad group dynamics. I didn't want any of them getting it into her head that she was my favorite. But because when all was said and done I was the boss, even though we were theoretically equal partners, every month, after splitting the take, I demanded that Nicoletta give me a first-class blowjob. It was a good way of reminding her whose idea it had been. After all, it was a profitable little operation. At year's end, after expenses, I pocketed about a hundred thousand euros, but I was forced to plow about half of that sum back into the restaurant. La Nena had turned into a money pit. The economic downturn was having its effect, even though the Veneto was doing better than many other parts of the country. It was damned expensive to keep up certain standards of quality. My biggest expense was staff. To say nothing of the wine cellar. It wasn't like the good old days. Now even people who could afford the finest still avoided the more expensive bottles. Only when bribers and bribees were drinking to the success of a negotiation was price truly no object. And they were demanding. Especially the ones who had never been able to get a seat at the main table to shovel forkfuls of the angel food cake of corruption into their gaping maws: they always seemed to know all about the latest fashions in wine. I made sure I always had plenty of the latest thing in stock.

Nothing on earth could have convinced me to give up La Nena. It was solid proof that my life had changed for good, a calling card that gave me a respected status in society. In the year 2000, thanks to Brianese and his hefty fee, I obtained legal rehabilitation. My personal history as a former terrorist sentenced to life imprisonment without parole was expunged from my record. At the end of a long and twisted series of events, during which I'd worked like a mule, I had become an upright citizen and the proprietor of a fashionable establishment in the heart of a city in the Venetian provinces. I voted in elections and I paid my taxes. And with a series of smiles, ass-lickings, and lots of hard work, I won acceptance. I was now "one of them." And not just any one of them. I was a winner. One of the people you couldn't pretend you hadn't seen or forget to say hello to.

Nicoletta picked up on the third ring. With her voice made hoarse from too many cigarettes, she always sounded as if she'd just gotten out of bed.

"How many and where?" she asked.

"All four, and tonight they don't have to travel."

"Understood. I'll get them ready."

I went to take their orders. Brianese had already put his guests at their ease and was explaining how he could intervene to help them win a number of contracts for school and army barracks renovations in a neighboring province. When I returned with the wine, they'd already struck a deal for a 3 percent cut and now they were talking about the right gifts to give each official. The building commissioner had made it known that he expected a year's worth of landscaping services.

Waiting for me at the bar was my wife, Martina, fiddling with her aperitif glass. I gave her a smile and a kiss on the lips—lips that tasted of Campari.

"Ciao, darling."

Then I said hello to Gemma, the friend who had come in with her, and pointed to a table where a well dressed, austere-looking gentleman was dining alone. "Do you mind eating with Professor Salvini? He's the new chief pediatrician, he's just moved to town, and he doesn't know anybody."

The doctor was glad to welcome them to his table. Knowing Gemma, I assumed that within five minutes she'd know all about the physician's personal life. She'd been on the prowl for a stable relationship ever since her husband dumped her and moved south to the Salento district of Puglia, where he now lived with his new girlfriend. Luckily, Martina could step in and keep Gemma from taking things too far. Martina and I had been married for nine years and she came in every day to eat lunch and dinner at my place. The kitchen in our apartment was used only for breakfast in the morning and for an infrequent herbal tea at night. If it was up to her, Martina would have been thrilled to cook meals and host lunches and dinners for friends and relatives, but I always opposed the idea vehemently. I didn't see the point of getting a bunch of pots and pans dirty when there was an excellent restaurant available. The waitress came over to ask what my wife would be having this evening. I always ordered for her. I did my best to take care of every aspect of her life. It was my way of showing her how much I loved her. And how grateful I was to her. She'd been there for me at one of the most difficult points in my life, when Roberta, the woman I was about to marry, died suddenly. A tragic accident snatched her away from me. She had an aspirin allergy, and she'd accidentally ingested a fatal overdose at my house. Because of my past, and due to unfounded suspicions on the part of her parents and the parish priest, whom Roberta considered her spiritual guide, I was investigated for murder and persecuted by two overzealous noncommissioned Carabinieri officers. I was lucky that Counselor Brianese stepped in and settled the case. My fiancée had actually introduced me to Martina. At the time, Martina was dating a guy with a poncey accent. Even though we were both involved with other people, something clicked between us and we had a meaningless little fling. It may have been meaningless but it did give me a useful piece of information: unlike my bride-to-be Roberta, Martina was passionate in bed. I saw her again at the funeral; she was at my side the whole time, consoling me and holding my hand.

A few months later, by the time my grief over Roberta's death had faded into a giant blank, we started dating and one night I asked her to marry me.

Actually, I was just planning to live with her, but Brianese had insisted on a proper marriage. That way, people would be more likely to forget about my past and about Roberta. I entrusted the logistics and details of the happiest day of our lives to Nicoletta and everything went off without a hitch. Refined, a little dull for most of the guests, and exhausting for the newlyweds. My lawyer was my best man and Gemma was Martina's maid of honor.

When we got back from our honeymoon in Polynesia we moved to the new house, not far from La Nena and, as we had solemnly vowed, we started taking care of one another.

The first thing I did was advise Martina to quit her job. Her monthly salary of 1,500 euros wouldn't change a thing in our lives and it would only come between us. She didn't want to stop working at first but in the end I convinced her that it was the best thing to do. She was mostly worried that she'd be bored.

"That'll never happen, my love."

Just like any other couple, getting to know one another and accepting the shortcomings of your spouse was a challenge, but we were in love and in the end we overcame every hurdle. One of the biggest challenges was Gemma and I'd been forced to play my cards with great cunning to curb her negative influence over my wife. Martina had always told me every last detail about her best friend and I knew that things weren't going well in her marriage at that time. So, with admirable generosity, I'd helped her to find a new apartment, a job, and a good lawyer. When Gemma came to thank me I made it clear to her that the time had come for her to be a friend to both of us. I needed an ally to help me maintain a balance in our happy married life.

"I don't like what I'm hearing," she said. "I've been close to Martina since middle school. She's my best friend, and you're just an acquaintance to me . . . "

I raised one hand to stop her. "If I tell her to stop seeing you for good, she'll do as I say. And right now you don't have any other best friends, or even a man, for that matter."

"Martina doesn't have any other close friends either," she shot back in annoyance.

"But I can buy her all the friends I want and I can deprive you of everything you have."

Gemma turned pale and bit her lip to keep from crying, but I hastened to add: "I'm not looking for a fight. But you know that Martina has a complicated personality and she needs time to wrap her mind around certain concepts."

"So you want me to help convince her that you're always right."

"Gemma, I *am* always right. I work all day, year round, and I need someone to go on vacation with her . . . Winters, summers, weekends . . . all expenses paid, of course."

"I wish I could just tell you to go fuck yourself," she said under her breath.

I gave her an affectionate pat on the cheek. "But you won't do that because I'm making your life easier and more comfortable. Look at yourself: you smoke too much, you're overweight, you always drink at least one spritz too many, you're obviously unhappy, and without Martina and her adorable husband, you'll only go downhill."

At that point, true to the script, she tried to justify herself, find a reason to be able to look herself in the face in the bathroom mirror every morning. "But you do love her at least?"

"I'm crazy about her. Why else do you think I'd behave in such an odious fashion? Because I can't afford to lose her."

And for once I'd told the truth, even if it was just a line from an old movie. Living with Martina, taking care of her had brought a little peace into my life, but most importantly it had laid to rest those impulses I'd been unable to control in the past and that still surfaced now and then, even though I no longer needed to get drunk on violence and cruelty in order to feel I was alive.

The cell phone rang. It was Nicoletta. "All set."

"I'll go give the clients the good news."

I walked into the back room and signaled to Brianese, who was entertaining his new business partners with gossip about the adventures of the Padanos in Rome. He stood up and with great solemnity, as if he were about to address the Italian parliament, he announced: "And now, gentlemen, it is my pleasure to introduce you to several lovely young ladies who can't wait to attend to the needs of our insatiable cocks."

The developers burst into a vulgar belly laugh, far too enthusiastic for such a feeble joke. The Counselor led them out of the back room, and then turned around to look back at me. The smile vanished from his lips.

"I'll be back tomorrow night. Like I said, we need to talk."

"Did something happen?"

He flashed a bitter grimace disguised as a smile: "Something always happens."

On his way out he stopped to say hello to Martina and to be introduced to Professor Salvini, whose center-left sympathies were well known. Brianese was polite but brisk. After all, he was certainly more interested in the time he was about to spend with the whore who was waiting for him than the time he might waste on some guy who would never vote for him.

My wife came over to me a few minutes later while I was

adding up a check at the cash register. She showed me a CD. "I want to play this for Gemma."

For a few seconds I paid close attention to the music issuing from the speakers. It was an instrumental version of Lucio Battisti's *Il mio canto libero.*

"It's nothing weird, is it?" I asked in a low voice. "Like political protest songwriters or jazz laments or ethnic wailing?"

She smiled. "Don't worry. It's a French group, I won't chase your customers away."

I reached out my hand and looked at her. She didn't have a single honey-blonde hair out of place, her makeup was perfect, her string of pearls, her blouse amply filled by her breasts, just lightly retouched by the plastic surgeon. The scars were still evident and I loved to run my tongue around their outlines. Martina was beautiful, serious, practically perfect. I took a quick look at the clock on the wall. That evening I felt like hurrying home early to be with her.

As I suspected, the music of the French group wasn't suited to La Nena's style and clientele. It was an unholy marriage of *chanson française*, old-time swing, and world music. Martina was adorable but she really didn't know shit about music. By the third track, when the biggest producer of poultry manure in the province gestured for me to change the music, I hit the off switch and replaced the CD with the latest release by Giusy Ferreri.

At eleven o'clock on the dot my wife stood up, shook hands with Salvini, and came over with Gemma to say goodnight.

"Don't be late," she whispered in my ear.

"We're changing the dinner menu tomorrow night and I have to talk to the cook, but I'll do my best to make it quick."

Gemma helped her into her floor-length down coat.

"Do you feel like taking a walk?"

"Yes," I said, answering for her. "Martina has a couple of glasses of Amarone she needs to metabolize."

The head physician signaled for the check. I brought it over to him in person, along with a snifter of cognac from my personal stock.

He shoved his nose into the snifter. "What a bouquet! I really shouldn't drink any more this evening, but there are delights that you can't turn down."

He sampled it like a connoisseur. "Excellent!"

I smiled and turned to go.

"Maybe this will help me to make a decision that I can't put off any longer."

"Have you decided to stay on as head physician?"

He shook his head. "I'm just filling in until the Freemasons and the Communion and Liberation Party can come to an agreement. No, the decision has to do with a little patient of mine . . . "

"This cognac is infallible," I said brusquely, cutting the conversation short. His confidence had made me uncomfrotable.

My tone wasn't lost on Salvini. He shot me a sidelong glance and set his snifter down on the table. "I'll pay with a credit card. Please add a 10 percent tip for the waiters," he announced with some considerable resentment.

I had just lost a customer. That wasn't so bad. Clearly he'd failed to understand that the services I offered didn't include friendly pats on the back.

The apartment, dimly lit by the diffuse lights scattered here and there between the entrance and the hallway, was shrouded in silence. It seemed as if there was nobody there but I knew exactly where Martina was. I stepped into the walk-in closet, took off my shoes, and put them with the other shoes set aside for cleaning. My wife would take care of them. Everything that concerned me personally was her responsibility. I would never have allowed our housekeeper to touch my things. Then my jacket, tie, and trousers wound up hanging on a clothes valet that, considering how much it cost me, deserved a place in our living room. Underwear and socks went into the laundry hamper. I walked naked into the bedroom and sat down in an armchair positioned so as to give me a complete view of the bathroom, which was lit up brightly. It looked like a film set. Martina was nude too, standing next to the bathroom sink. From a glass shelf she picked up various jars and bottles of creams and ointments, opened them, and set them down in a precise order. She stuck her fingers into the first jar and then rubbed them over her face with slow circular movements. More cream went onto her neck and her hands never stopped moving, slowly descending until they reached her feet. She put the jars back onto the shelf. Then, with a graceful motion, she lifted her left leg and braced her foot on the edge of the sink. Her middle finger traced the outlines of her public hair, which her beautician had razored into the shape of the initial of my first name. Then her finger was swallowed up by her labia majora as she searched for her clitoris. I waited until her eyelids fluttered shut and she started breathing in short labored pants.

"That's enough."

Martina kept touching herself. "Oh, please, I'm almost there."

"I said that's enough."

She moved her hand away. "But why?"

"That CD was a piece of shit. You disrespected me."

She was about to come back at me with an answer of some kind, but then she changed her mind. She shut the door with one foot, slamming it ever so slightly.

I put on my silk pajamas and slipped into bed. A few minutes later Martina got in beside me. I wrapped my arms around her in a hug.

"Good night, my love."

I woke up perfectly rested. My wife, as usual, was already

up. I couldn't stand the idea of waking up with a disheveled woman sleeping beside me, with puffy eyes and morning breath, shuffling around the house in her slippers. Martina was in the kitchen, in her morning outfit: skirt, blouse, ballet flats, a hint of makeup, one or two pieces of jewelry.

Breakfast was ready.

"I wanted to apologize for last night," she said in a small voice. "I'd listened to the CD in the car and thought it was pretty."

I took her face in my hands. "Let's forget it ever happened," I announced before planting a kiss on her lips.

As she was pouring my coffee I walked over to the refrigerator and pulled a sheet of paper off a magnet shaped like a strawberry.

"This morning you have an hour of pilates and your massage. After lunch you're having your teeth cleaned. And that's all?" I asked in surprise.

"Going to the dentist wears me out, you know that. Afterwards I'd prefer to stay in and just watch some television."

"Understood. But the whole afternoon strikes me as excessive. Get a nice hour's run in between six and seven o'clock, okay?"

"It's cold out," she whined.

"Christ, Martina, do we have to argue about every last detail of our life together?"

"I'm sorry, you're right."

She handed me the demitasse cup. I drank slowly, sipping the coffee and savoring it to the last drop. Then I took the tablets of vitamin supplements and laid them out on the table alongside her glass of orange juice. With her customary gesture, she reached out, picked them up, and popped them into her mouth. Essential trace elements, antioxidants, tonics . . . the finest products on the market in terms of slowing or ward-ing off the aging process and keeping body and mind in tip-top shape. I purchased them over the Internet after selecting them personally. Every Sunday I read the special supplement of a major national daily newspaper in search of articles with useful information for my beloved Martina.

She spread jam on the melba toast and started talking. Breakfast was the one time of the day when I listened to anything she wanted to tell me. It was important for her. She constantly needed attention and advice.

Nicoletta warned me before I married her: "This one still hasn't figured out who you really are. If you want to hold onto her, you'd better make sure she never does."

"Any advice?"

"Pretend to listen to her, to be deeply absorbed in all her problems. She's the classic woman who needs to have a give-and-take dialogue with her man."

"What about you?" I asked with a smile.

"I'm smarter than that, handsome. In my first year of high school I figured out what a waste of time that is."

I took her advice, and it worked. Every morning Martina entertained me for a solid half hour with her bullshit. She talked about her family, Gemma, other girlfriends that meant less to her, acquaintances, anecdotes, gossip, various purchases, and finally, the two of us. The endless source of anxiety in that period was her father's illness. Another old guy enlisted by cruel fate in the Alzheimer's battalion. She wanted to spend more time with her mother and her sisters, and she was afraid of what they thought of her. From the very beginning I'd made it perfectly clear that children and in-laws were not subjects I cared to engage in. I wasn't born to dandle infants on my knee or to spend Sundays, Easters, and Christmases seated at long, noisy tables full of in-laws. I'd turned my back on my own family years ago and I didn't miss them in the slightest.

"I know you too well," I told her that morning. "You'd

become sad and unsightly, because grief gives you wrinkles and creases; that's what the surgeon told you when he did your eyelid surgery. And you'd be ruining your life for nothing, because there's nothing that you can do. Your father's done for. And there are already lots of people taking care of him."

She grabbed my hand. "I'm begging you. Three times a week. I need to be close to my mama and to Paola and Romina."

"You've already got so many things scheduled . . . "

"I'll take care of everything. I swear it."

I lifted her hands to my lips and kissed them. "You're a good girl," I whispered in admiration. "I'm proud of you."

"Does that mean you'll let me?"

"As long as it doesn't affect our life together and, in any case, as long as you understand clearly that this is a major concession and I'll expect you to make one in return."

She threw her arms around my neck, deeply moved. "I love you."

"I love you, too."

At the end of a dull day, the lawyer and, incidentally, parliamentarian of the Italian republic Sante Brianese came back to La Nena at aperitif time to talk to me, as promised. After the standard salutations, and after downing a couple of glasses of bubbly, he waved me over.

"We'd better talk in the back room . . . is it clean?"

"Of course. I had it swept this morning."

"Good. Bring the bottle and a tray of hors d'oeuvres." The fad of bugging offices was a new one in the city. Bugs had been found in the offices of businessmen vying for contracts of various kinds, and the thing that had aroused the greatest alarm in certain circles was the fact that it probably hadn't been the police or investigating magistrates who had placed the bugs. A number of rumors were circulating about the likely provenance of these listening devices. Since Brianese was exposed to considerable risk and had a fair number of enemies, he'd hired a technician who worked in the sector to sweep the back room and other "sensitive" places in the bar.

Of course I'd had the rooms shielded against electronic eavesdroppers. There were idiots who complained that in the back room "I can't get a cell phone signal," but somehow they figured that no one would ever think to eavesdrop on them or wiretap them, and so I had to take care of things properly, if only to protect myself.

Along with the bottle of wine I brought a tray of local cold cuts and salamis and pickled vegetables. When he wasn't being forced to masquerade as the successful professional he'd become, and therefore an innovative and discerning gourmet, Brianese went back to being the son of the peasant farmer who broken his back to send him to the university.

He twisted and turned, talking with his mouth full of food about the responsibilities of "leaders." "This is a country where one minute the people adore you and the next minute they'll line you up against a wall in Piazzale Loreto and shoot you, or throw coins at you as you leave your hotel."

I speared an artichoke preserved in oil and a slice of salami with a toothpick and laid them down on a thin slice of bread.

"You're worrying me, Counselor. You're dragging this thing out a little too long for it not to be something serious."

He heaved a deep sigh and went straight to the point. "The whole Dubai business went belly-up. They screwed us with a Ponzi scheme."

I've never been a financial genius so I've always entrusted my money to Brianese and his expert advisers, but I wasn't a big enough fool to be taken in by that old trick. Like every other investor, large and small, on the planet, I'd followed the Madoff case with interest and I knew perfectly well that there were successors to Charles Ponzi around every corner, looking for idiots to fleece. They promise high returns on small investments but it's nothing more than a financial pyramid scheme. The few at the top of the pyramid rake in the cash invested by the many at the base, and on it would go until the hordes of chickens rushing in for the plucking begin to thin out.

"Even the English advisers who recommended that we get into the deal were screwed," he went on. "They flew out to Dubai but, instead of construction sites for luxury hotel and office towers, they just found a lot of old ditches. Those fucking Bedouins didn't even bother to pretend to build anything. Our friends tried to kick up a fuss but the authorities just loaded them onto the first plane out."

According to what Brianese had promised me, I was going to be the owner of two mini-apartments on the sixteenth floor of an exclusive skyscraper and a suite in a hotel for billionaires. "Any hope of getting the money back?" I asked, even though I already knew the answer.

"None. The con was organized far too high up the ladder. They've already pulled the strings that need to be pulled. It ends here. The media have talked about it but without too much emphasis, because we don't have any real interest in showing how deeply we're involved in this thing . . . "

I nodded as I looked him straight in the eye. Brianese snapped in annoyance: "Don't look at me like that, goddamn it! You saw the commercials on Dubai television yourself."

"How much do I have left?"

"Nothing."

"Nothing? But you assured me you were going to invest part of my money in that real estate deal in Croatia . . . I remember you partied big time when the deal went through."

"I had to make room for other people and I had to leave you out. I need allies even outside the party," he admitted with an edge of embarrassment. "But don't worry about it, you'll make it back. Your prostitution ring takes in plenty of cash and when you've put together another pile of money, let's say, half a million euros, I'll slip you into a safe investment. For example, after the regional elections they're going to announce the route for the new high-speed train line. I have a way of finding out about it in advance, so that we can buy up a nice parcel of low-cost farmland and then resell it at three times the price."

I shook my head, with a forced smile stamped on my face to conceal the seething astonishment and rage. "No, Counselor, that's not the way it works. I gave you two million and two million is what I want back. All these years you've managed my money and taken a 10 percent cut, on top of what you earned by managing my capital. That's your problem if you let someone rip you off."

"Business always entails a certain risk factor," he replied in a paternal tone of voice. "Sometimes you make more money, sometimes you make less, and sometimes things turn sour and you lose everything. Just deal with it and think about the future."

He went on yakking and stuffing his face with food and wine, as if I was just the least of his many voters or one of his idiot clients to whom he was explaining that it wasn't his fault that the case went against them. I earned that money by risking my neck in an armed robbery where I was the sole survivor and in a number of other deals that could easily have cost me prison time. The lawyer and parliamentarian Sante Brianese had simply kept the money that I'd lost and distributed it to himself and his friends, gobbling it up along with the contracts, the bribes, the stock swaps, the illicit favors, the fake consulting fees, in other words, all the best aspects of modern politics in Italy.

I'd figured out the way it worked some time ago, ever since the days when he'd convinced me to invest in loan sharking, a sector that the Counselor had abandoned once his political successes catapulted him into the paradise of public works contracts, projects that became bigger and more expensive every year. The Veneto region had become one enormous construction site and the river of cash flowing across the countryside was so immense that at a certain point it became necessary to invest the money outside of the country. In Croatia and Dubai, for instance. Brianese didn't manage those investments personally. His role was to find the money. Then he entrusted it to certain experts whose names he'd always taken great care not to reveal.

And the experts can go fuck themselves too, I thought to myself.

"Counselor, please forgive me, but you've got it wrong," I interrupted in a placid tone of voice. "I can meet you partway on this and give you your usual commission of 200,000 euros, but the rest of my capital has to come back to me."

"Oh, then, you really are an idiot!"

"Excuse me?"

"You heard me loud and clear," he hissed furiously. "If you're anybody at all today the credit is all mine. I cleared your criminal record, I got you out of hot water when they were trying to send you to jail for Roberta's death, I arranged for you to buy this restaurant, I honored you by appearing as your best man at your wedding, I've helped you make excellent investments year after year, and now you dare to speak to me in this fashion?"

I took a deep breath. This wasn't the time to lose my temper. "I certainly had a great debt of gratitude to you, Counselor. You did a lot for me over the years, but I always paid you back. And I'm not just talking about the money I paid you. What with your fees and the commissions that you took on my investments, it comes to a considerable sum. There was a time when I worked as an enforcer for you and your friends. I broke bones and silenced people who could have gotten you into some deep trouble."

He swept his hand through the air with dismissive anger. "That's yesterday's news," he shouted. "We were younger then, more reckless and less powerful."

I ignored his bullshit response. "I put together a ring of prostitutes that I ought to patent, it's so foolproof, and we both know how much trouble you're causing yourself by this idea of yours of putting pussy on the top of the maypole. And La Nena has always been at your complete disposal: dinners, campaign parties, aperitif parties to introduce the candidates, and you never paid a cent. I'd like to know how much money you've made doing business in this back room that I have swept every week at my own expense . . . "

He grabbed my wrist to stop me and changed his tone of voice.

"You're right, I apologize. In all these years we've helped each other out and we both benefited from it. You're a smart boy and you have all my esteem and affection and that's why you have to believe me when I tell you that I don't owe you a penny—"

"I find it difficult to believe you, especially when I think of the fact that you kept me out of the Croatian deal."

He spread his arms wide. "I already explained why that had to happen. The Fearless Leader is increasingly at risk of making a crash landing, and we have to brace ourselves for impact if that happens, so we can survive the end of his rule and go on governing. This is the time to reach out and make new alliances and develop new strategies."

"Talk to me about money, Counselor. It's the only subject I'm interested in."

He sighed. "All right, all right! I give you my word that, within a year from today, I'll reimburse you for your loss with 25 percent interest."

"That strikes me as a pretty daunting commitment," I replied, baffled.

He refilled our glasses and raised his in a toast. "Just remember who I am and what my word is worth."

I picked up my glass and accepted his toast. Brianese got to his feet.

"Duty calls, I have a party meeting to decide on the upcoming candidates."

"Good luck."

"I'm going to need it," he muttered as he pulled a box of mints out of his jacket pocket and tossed a couple into his mouth.

Brianese was an intelligent, skillful, pragmatic man. I'd always respected those qualities of his and I ought to have been satisfied with the way he'd come around on the two million euros, but there was something that didn't add up. I had the feeling that his final toast of farewell, offered as a guarantee of his promise, was just dictated by his haste to win over the latest asshole in a long succession of suckers. It didn't strike me as being in keeping with his style. My doubts became intolerable over the course of the next half hour, and when I caught myself being rude and abusive to the chef for no good reason, even though I know how hard it is to find good cooks in this city, I decided to make a phone call to a person who might be able to help clear up my lingering misgivings. He was willing to meet me but since I couldn't very well show up empty-handed I gave Nicoletta a call.

"Do you have a couple of girls free?"

"Yes. The two Venezuelans."

"I'll swing by to pick them up."

A moment of silence ensued. "For personal use?"

"I need to give a gift."

"Understood."

"This is a useful investment for the company," I lied. "Anyway, I'll take care of the girls."

I made a quick round of the tables and I took a seat at the

one where Martina and Gemma were sitting. Gemma hastened to point out the absence of Professor Salvini.

"He didn't make a reservation tonight," I explained. "He must have moved on to try the cooking in some other restaurant. Anyway, I doubt we'll see him in here again. He said that he wasn't used to spending so much for a meal. The classic bullshit you hear from the radical chic crowd."

Martina smiled at the cutting comment. I ordered a grilled tenderloin with a side of roasted vegetables.

"How'd your run go?" I asked.

"It went great. My time's improving."

I caressed her cheek and turned to Gemma. "She's prettier with every day that passes, don't you think?"

"She has the good luck of having a man who loves her to distraction." I shot her a warning glance not to exaggerate, but Martina blushed slightly as she nodded: "It's true. I really am a lucky girl."

I stood up. "I have to leave you two. There's a wine tasting outside of town and I'm running late."

I left Piero, the oldest waiter, in charge of the place and headed for the garage where I lovingly kept my Phaeton, a full-size sedan made by Volkswagen. It never sold well, though it's a luxury vehicle and priced accordingly, at over 100,000 euros. I bought it for a ridiculously low price from a client who was in a hurry to get rid of it before leaving the country and moving to Bulgaria, where he now lives in a handsome villa overlooking the Black Sea, out of the reach of creditors and the tax authorities. He sold cell phones to the tune of 20 million euros out of a fake shell company based in Burgas, Bulgaria. That little scam allowed him to become one of the many total tax evaders who make the economy of the Veneto as successful as it is.

He invited me to step outside La Nena and showed me the car. "It's got five thousand kilometers on it. You can have it for 30,000 euros."

I shook my head. "I have 20,000 on hand. I can't get any more than that tomorrow or the next day. I might be able to get 30,000 in ten days or so . . . maybe."

He tossed me the keys. "You just got a bargain."

No doubt about it. And now I was driving a handcrafted jewel with refined and understated lines. Exactly the kind of car that makes you look good in certain circles in the Veneto.

After a ten-minute drive I pulled up in front of a small villa on the immediate outskirts of the city. A new development surrounded by bypasses and beltways and completely devoid of infrastructure.

Nicoletta was waiting for me with the two girls in front of a crackling wood fire. They were relaxed, smoking cigarettes.

"Damn, Nicoletta, it really is a shame you have to ruin that perfume with those cigarettes," I said, as I leaned down to plant a kiss on her cheek. "It's incredible and it gave me a hard-on the nanosecond I smelled it."

Isabel and Dulce snickered. Nicoletta pretended she hadn't heard me.

"Where are you taking them this fine evening?" she asked in a low voice.

"To work in a factory."

"Another industrialist who can't seem to have sex outside of his office?"

"Something like that."

"If you get them back to me by a decent hour tonight I have a couple of Englishmen parked at the spa who would be glad of their company."

"I'll do what I can. Where are the other two?"

"In Venice. I'm driving to pick them up tomorrow morning."

The sign and the lights in the offices were all dark. The security guard at the front gate pointed me to a large industrial shed. I parked near the entrance and told the girls to get out of the car. "Is this the right place?" Dulce asked in a worried tone.

"Yes it is, so now shut up and put on a smile."

We walked into an immense printing plant. The presses and other machinery were all still and silent but, in a lighted area, thirty or so men, standing along a worktable, were hand-assembling advertising leaflets for a supermarket. They worked in silence, focusing on the rhythm with which they lifted and folded the sheets of paper. They had their backs to us and didn't even notice we were there until they heard the unmistakable sound of the girls' six-inch heels. They swung around suddenly and stared at us in surprise. There were lots of things that wouldn't have surprised them that evening, but the arrival of two such stunning beauties wasn't one of them.

A stocky powerfully built figure emerged out of the darkness, a man dressed in a 20-euro fleece pullover, shapeless trousers, and running shoes. He took one last drag on his cigarette and dropped it on the floor.

"Well, what are you looking at?" he shouted. All the men turned around and went back to work.

"I didn't expect you to show up with lovely company," he said as we shook hands, gauging the girls with an expert eye. "My name's Domenico," he introduced himself. "And you two lovely young ladies?"

His last name was Beccaro. He was the owner of a printing company that his father had founded with two shabby old printing presses that now enjoyed pride of place alongside the giant oak-and-steel desk in his office. Domenico had worked hard and played his cards right with a few local politicians. I first met him at La Nena when he came to a few dinners in the back room with Brianese, invariably followed by entertainment in the company of my girls. Then he came back to eat with his wife and a few friends and told me that my menus weren't very well printed, and that I should come to see him sometime. So I did and he became my trusted printer. The menu work I gave him from the restaurant was nothing compared to the orders he got from corporations and restaurant chains, but he was one of those businessmen who never turn away a customer. He spoke exclusively in dialect but he managed to make himself perfectly understood in every walk of life. Months ago, by pure coincidence, I overheard a snatch of conversation as I was opening a bottle of wine that let me know that he too had been involved in the Dubai deal. Now I'd come to see him in hopes that by offering him the services of my girls I could get him to tell me how much money he'd lost on the deal and how he hoped to get it back. My partner always gathered information about our clients. She claimed that one day it might prove useful. And in her dossier on Domenico Beccaro she had him coded under the heading *t.c.h.*: total cunt hound.

"So how did you happen to be passing through my neck of the woods?" he asked as he continued to exchange happy smiles with Isabel and Dulce.

"Like I said on the phone, I just happened to be around here with my two young friends and I thought I'd invite you to have a drink and chat about a certain investment opportunity I have in mind. I never thought you'd still be at work at this hour."

"Carissimo, we never stop working here. By day we print and by night we fold and collate."

"By hand? Wouldn't it make more sense to buy machinery?"

"You're crazy!" he blurted out. "It costs me less to have these guys do the job. I've always thought of myself as a benefactor."

He caught my smile and turned serious. "I'm not joking. They really love me, believe it."

"I don't doubt it. But do you really have to stay here?"

"Yeah, all night. It's just me and the security guard, but we can chat if you like," he said, linking arms with me. "Man, your friends are mighty hot, I have to say."

"Oh, they're friendly and warmhearted, too."

"I'd love to show them around my office if I didn't have to stay here to keep an eye on things. You turn your back for five minutes and they start fucking off and the next thing you know you're losing customers, you know how it is . . . "

"I could keep an eye on them, if you like . . . "

"For real?"

"Of course. We can talk about the deal some other time. I've heard good things about certain investments in Dubai . . . "

"Leave that alone, it's old news."

"What do you mean?"

"It's a scam that was blown wide open in early June," he explained. "I almost fell for it myself, with a group of investors. Luckily we found out in time and rerouted our money into other opportunities."

"Really?"

Domenico was in a hurry to end the conversation so he could dedicate himself body and soul to the two girls. He said more than he should have. "Ask Brianese about it," he said brusquely. "He knows all the details."

A wave of fury passed from the tips of my toes to the ends of my hair, and immediately subsided, giving way to a wash of bitterness. I couldn't seem to take in the fact that the Counselor had chosen to screw me this way.

I smiled at Beccaro and turned to my girls. "My friend wants to show you his office."

Domenico took the two girls by the hand and walked off, making it clear to his gang of blue-collar workers that he was about to have sex with a pair of spectacular hookers. Isabel turned to look back at me for instructions and I fanned out both hands, showing her all ten fingers. That was how many minutes of sex they were supposed to give him.

I ignored the promise I'd made to keep an eye on those losers. I got the car and drove around to the front door of the offices. Motionless, both hands on the steering wheel, I did my best to calm down, even though I knew the only way I'd find inner peace was in the intoxicating thrill of inflicting pain on others. Martina. She'd understand me and her love would give me a sense of relief. Only after that would I be capable of restoring some semblance of order to my mind.

Domenico accompanied the girls to the car. A freshly lit cigarette dangled from his lip. He leaned down to the driver's side window. "Thanks for coming to see me," he said.

"Drop by La Nena to say hello. I have a couple of new wines you ought to try."

"He reeked of sweat," Dulce complained from the passenger seat.

"I need a shower," Isabel piled on.

"You can get cleaned up at the spa. Two clients are waiting for you there."

"But we're only supposed to work once a day," Dulce objected.

I gripped the steering wheel tighter to keep from giving her the back of my hand. "You can make an exception this once," I said in a conciliatory tone. "After all, these are two clean, nice smelling gentlemen with good manners, and you'll be entertaining them in big comfortable beds in a luxury hotel. But if you open your mouths one more time to complain I'll take you straight back to that printing plant and toss you to that band of miserable laborers."

Both girls fell silent and, when I pulled up in front of Nicoletta's small villa, they shot out of the car in a hurry.

It wasn't late and La Nena was still humming at that time of night, but the restaurant was the last thing on my mind that night. When I got home Martina was stretched out on the sofa in the living room. She had a book in her hands and the voice of a singer-songwriter was pouring out of the speakers. The music had drowned out any other noises and she hadn't noticed when I got home. I stood there watching her. When she read she got a thoughtful look on her face, as if every word demanded her full attention. She was wearing a light woolen dress that left her thighs uncovered.

I went into my office to do a little Internet research about the Dubai scam. Beccaro was right: it was old news. Brianese really did think I was a pathetic imbecile.

I went to take off my clothes, then I walked back to the living room and sat down at the edge of the sofa. She smiled and put a hand on my chest. "I'm sorry, I didn't hear you come in. I'll hurry into the bathroom and get the creams ready."

"No," I whispered. "Spinning, baby, spinning."

She turned pale. "What happened?"

I led her by the hand to a room that contained only a spinner bike and, next to it, a large, cushy, comfortable oxblood red leather armchair. I took off her dress with a single movement. She was trembling. I unhooked her bra.

"At least tell me what happened, I beg you . . . "

"Get up on that fucking bicycle," I shouted.

She obeyed and started pedaling. I sank back into the armchair, enjoying the contact of my naked flesh with the leather.

I snapped my fingers to indicate the pace she should pedal at and I sat there listening to the sound of the spinning roller as it gobbled up imaginary miles. After a while I started to relex. Martina was already glistening with sweat, her hair matted to her temples. She kept her eyes shut tight in order to maintain her focus. After a while, I closed mine too to find answers to the thousand questions that were crowding into my mind. I never dreamed that I'd find myself on a collision course with Sante Brianese, my lawyer, the best man at my wedding, and until that evening, something like a father to me. I felt betrayed, embittered, and defeated. As well as confused. I didn't have the slightest idea of how to behave.

Suddenly I noticed that my wife was slowing down the pace of her pedaling. I leapt to my feet and started insulting her with meticulous cruelty. I spared her nothing until she choked back her tears and returned to her starting speed.

I sat down again and it dawned on me that I had no desire to break off ties with Brianese. I had to find a way to make him repent the error of his ways, realize that he had wronged me and make things right. There was a time when I would have handled things differently and the Counselor would have been dead by now. In my mind there was a jumble of faces, the faces of people I'd run into on my way to leading a normal life, people who were no longer around. But I wasn't a criminal living on the margins of society now, and Brianese was a member of parliament. We were all respectable citizens and only constructive dialogue could smooth out our disagreements.

Martina suddenly stopped and collapsed, without strength, sliding off the spinner bike like a rag doll and falling to the floor with a faint thud. I looked down at her as she lay panting, her chest jerking fitfully, and it dawned on me what the best approach might be in my bid to get the Counselor's attention.

"Fuck me," she murmured. "Please, come fuck me."

I pulled down her panties and slid into her. She wrapped her arms around my neck with what strength remained to her. "I'm here, my love. I'm here for you."

Sante Brianese lived in an elegant two-story townhouse adjoining one of the gates of the medieval city walls. Over the years I had stockpiled sufficient information to be confident that in the mornings, his wife was the first to leave the house. She went to work at the small fashion design company she owned, which she had refused to give up even though she no longer needed to work for a living. When the Counselor wasn't in Rome, he left the house a short while later, heading either for the hall of justice or to his law office. The couple's two daughters were grown up now and had left home years ago. The older daughter was married to an ambitious young diplomat and the younger one was in London where she was working on her MBA.

When I rang the doorbell I was certain that nobody would be home but the housekeeper. The sunny day justified the sunglasses I was wearing. To complete my disguise I was wearing a cap with a visor and a jacket that might be taken at a distance for the uniform of a shipping company. Under my arm I was carrying a large padded envelope.

In that house, couriers came and went all day long, so the woman opened the door to me without thinking twice. I slugged her hard with a right cross to the chin. I was wearing my brass knuckles so she was out like a light and flat on the floor before she could get a look at my face. I dragged her into the good living room and stretched her out on a damask sofa. Only then did I realize that she was wearing a maid's uniform, complete with white cloth tiara. I slipped on a pair of white latex gloves and began going through the home methodically in search of the master bedroom. I found it on the second floor and, as I expected, it was a triumph of antique furniture and paintings of the late-eighteenth-century Venetian school. I started pulling open dresser drawers and rummaging through the clothing, making it obvious that someone had touched everything. In the bathroom I went through the medicine cabinets and opened the perfume bottles and jars of creams and ointments, systematically violating the privacy of the owners of the house.

I found one of the Counselor's light raincoats in the armoire, ready to be worn when next fall rolled around. I pulled off the nylon dry cleaner bag and put the raincoat on, buttoning it up to my chin. It smelled as if it had been recently cleaned. I walked back downstairs. The housekeeper was still out cold. She was powerfully built, about forty-five. I slipped the brass knuckles back on and punched her in the face ten times or so, reducing it to a mask of blood. I ripped off her apron and dabbed at the wounds to evaluate the damage. Her left cheekbone was still intact. I pulled her lips open with two fingers. Most of her teeth were still in place. A diet that was short on sugar but high in vitamins and grains had made her teeth especially strong. She must have grown up in the countryside.

"Healthy peasant stock, my ass," I snarled in exasperation as I took aim, determined to finish the job properly. To keep her from drowning in her own blood I laid her out face down, bleeding onto an antique Sarouk Persian rug. I took off the raincoat, put it back into its clear plastic holder, and put it where it had been in the closet. As I was leaving I stopped to take one last look at the woman. I took the white maid's cap as a souvenir and left for work.

At the aperitif hour it was the only topic of conversation in the city. As more and more alcohol was consumed, the gory details of the attack became more gruesome.

"There were four of them, and they took turns raping her," the wife of a wholesaler in meats informed me. She was wearing an elegant silver fox fur coat.

"Bastards," I hissed indignantly. Brianese was too busy giving interviews to come in. This was a golden opportunity for him to hit all the standard themes that were so important to his party, such as the crisis in public safety and the problem of the gypsy camps, which were hotbeds of potential thieves and housebreakers. Knowing him, he'd make sure he got pictures to the reporters showing the devastating damage to the Ukrainian housekeepers's face, but he'd make sure nobody found out that someone had rummaged through his underwear and his wife's makeup and bras. He'd also have to lie about the motives for the attack, dreaming up some nonexistent motive for a burglary. The Counselor, as always, would rise to the occasion as he desperately tried to figure out who, out of the vast armies of his enemies, would have dared to impart such an unmistakable and alarming warning shot.

This was the beginning of a thought process that, with a little help from me, would lead him to understand that he had done wrong when he decided to rob me of two million euros.

Martina showed up solo. "What about Gemma?" I asked.

"She's not feeling well. She decided to stay home tonight."

Her eyes searched mine for any remaining traces of concern. She still couldn't understand what had happened the night before but she knew that whatever it was she couldn't ask for an explanation.

I signaled the bartender to make her an aperitif. I leaned over and placed my lips close to her ear. "Just give me time to get dinner started and then we'll go somewhere no one can find us and we'll have a pizza together."

A radiant smile lit up her face and I went back to taking care of my customers. Two reporters for the local daily that was politically aligned with Brianese brought fresh news. The housekeeper was still in no condition to talk to the police but the owners of the house had reported the theft of jewelry, cash, and a collection of ancient coins. The detectives were already hot on the trail of a band of Moldavian criminals. Apparently the woman had been involved with an ex-convict at some point in the past. The usual lead, prepackaged for public consumption, to toss a little red meat to the press and to reassure public opinion.

One of the two reporters emphasized the Honorable Brianese's generosity in making sure that the woman was seen by one of the foremost experts in facial trauma.

"Which means she must have been an illegal immigrant," a

bank director who had already defected to the Padanos joked in dialect.

The whole room burst into laughter and I took advantage of the hubbub to sneak out with Martina. We walked arm-in-arm down the porticoes, idly looking at the show windows.

"Women's boots aren't much to look at this year," I said with conviction, parroting a comment I'd heard one of my female customers utter as I walked by her table. That was something I often did when I didn't know what to talk about.

"The truth is that you have very traditional tastes." She pointed to a pair of knee-high boots. "For instance, I could only wear those in private."

"You can bet on that. I'd never let you leave the house with those monstrosities on your feet."

We continued to joke around once we got to the pizzeria. The proprietor came over to our table and thanked me for honoring his restaurant with my patronage. In a voice loud enough to be heard by the other tables I told him that he made the best pizza in town. After we'd finished exchanging amiable compliments, he sent out a sampling of mozzarella di bufala produced by his Uncle Alfonso and sun-dried tomatoes made by some other relative of his.

Martina ordered a beer. "We're not eating German sausage and potatoes," I pointed out under my breath. "A Fiano d'Avellino is really the best accompaniment for both the mozzarella and the calzone alla ricotta that you ordered."

"Your wife ordered wisely," broke in the waiter, who had a strong Neapolitan accent and sharp ears. "The pizza is first-rate here but the wine selection is limited . . . and after all most of our customers don't order wine."

"Fine, have the beer," I gave in. I looked around to see if there were any well known faces from the local wine and food circuit. I hated to be seen in public breaking the golden rules of good wine and fine cuisine.

I was updating Martina on the latest developments concerning the vicious attack in the Brianese home when she suddenly burst out with unexpected news.

"I quarreled with Gemma. She's not really sick at all."

"What did you fight about?"

"She's in love with you."

"Did she tell you that?"

"Yes. I've had my suspicions for a while but yesterday afternoon, on the phone, I forced her to admit it."

I took her hand. "And you got mad."

"That's not all. I'm feeling sad, too. She was my best friend."

"Why do you say 'was'?"

"I can't see her anymore," she told me. "I couldn't take the tension of being in constant contact with a woman who wants to steal my husband away from me."

I flashed her a smirk of astonishment.

"What?" she asked in annoyance.

"Look, can you imagine me fucking Gemma?" I asked with a laugh. "It's not nice of you to show such a low opinion of my tastes in women."

She bit her lower lip. I took advantage of the chance to double down. "You're a genuinely lovely, desirable woman. Gemma, well, isn't."

"I'm sorry. I'm being insecure, as usual."

I changed tone. "That's right. And I'd like you to think for a minute about how deeply offensive you've been to me with this complete lack of trust. Do you really think all someone needs to do is let me get a whiff of pussy and I'll start cheating on my wife? Do you have any idea how many beautiful women come into La Nena?"

She started to mumble excuses and sail off into tangled and senseless explanations. When I saw she was on the verge of tears I laid my silverware in my plate and looked her straight in the eye.

"I love you and I have no intention whatsoever of giving you up. Make peace with Gemma. It makes no sense to break up such a fine and lasting friendship for a passing crisis of insecurity."

"You're right," she stammered. "It's a good thing we talked it over. I'm so relieved."

And so was I. I needed to keep Gemma as my accomplice.

When I headed back to my restaurant, after my wife said goodbye and gave me a kiss on the lips, reminding me not to stay out late, I called that idiot friend of hers.

"What the hell do you think you're doing?"

"Why don't you come over and I'll show you?"

I hung up. She was drunk. A good sign. Then she'd be smitten with remorse, there would be streams of tears and useless words and everything would go back the way it was. Between the two of them. The real problem was that now I saw Gemma in a new light. I'd always been attracted by women in their forties afflicted with chronic fragility. In my other life, before my relationship with Martina, who represented the summit of perfection from that point of view, I'd broken into the personal lives of countless women, playing relentlessly unfair with their weaknesses and dragging them down into the abyss with me, leaving behind me nothing but smoking ruins or wreckage silent with the chill of death. With my boyish good looks and my old school gentlemanly manners, I was a past master at lying and acting out extended scripts. That kind of woman only figures things out long after the point of no return. To avoid temptation I'd set myself some rigorous rules: never to fraternize with the female clients and the waitresses in the restaurant. I'd always turned down the numerous offers of sexual relations. The monthly blowjob I let Nicoletta give me was just a reiteration of roles between business partners, but I'd never have dreamed of embarking on an affair with her. Among other things, she wasn't my type; she basically devoured her men and then spit out the few remaining bones. But now Gemma's emotional fragility had been served up on a silver platter and I had to do my best to rein in my imagination. I focused on my work. But it wasn't easy.

Three days later, when Sante Brianese walked into La Nena with his usual brisk, energetic stride, he was accorded a hero's welcome. He'd been so skillful at exploiting the situation that he'd managed to appear on all the news broadcasts, and especially on the afternoon shows, which were the ones with the highest viewership among his average voters. The tearjerking story of the poor Moldavian women with a disfigured face, and the way that he had reached into his own savings to ensure she received the best possible medical care, had stirred the hearts of all Italy. He'd made sure he was photographed and filmed at her bedside in the hospital. After all, years of delivering summations in court and political speeches on the campaign trail had honed his rhetorical skills to a gleaming edge.

I waited for the cluster of customers swirling around him to thin out, then I came out from behind the counter. I threw my arms around him in a transport of emotion and I whispered into his ear: "So there never really was a Dubai deal at all. It's a bad thing to cheat your friends, Counselor."

I felt his whole body stiffen. I pulled back just long enough to stare into his eyes round with shock and then I slipped the maid's white cloth tiara into the pocket of his overcoat. I walked back to the counter. By the time I turned around Brianese was slipping out the front door. He'd be back soon. I felt sure of it.

A few minutes later Martina poked her head in the door and waved for me to join her outside.

"What is it?"

"That fool Gemma is ashamed to come in," she explained, pointing to her.

Gemma was half-hidden behind the pillar of a portico. She was moving her feet as if she were dancing out of time to some unheard music, and she was greedily sucking down lungsful of tobacco smoke.

I walked over to her. "Look, I really don't know what . . . " she mumbled.

"Starting tomorrow morning, you quit smoking."

"Excuse me?"

"Didn't you say you were in love with me?" I replied in a harsh tone of voice. "I wouldn't deign to consider a woman who reeks of tobacco smoke. If you want to put yourself on the market you're going to have to straighten up and fly right."

I turned around and returned to Martina's side. "Everything's fine now, darling," I reassured her. "Your table's the one in the corner. You're going to have to eat in the company of a prosciutto producer from Montagnana and his wife, but they're lovely people, you'll both like them."

Gemma avoided my eyes all evening. Her mind had been turned inside out. The next move was up to her. On the one hand, I hoped that she'd throw the door open to me, so I could take control of her life and pillage her self-respect. On the other hand, part of me hoped she wouldn't do it. That would be the last thing I needed, now that I'd opened a hotline with Brianese on the matter of the two million euros.

I would have bet anything that the Counselor would come back in person but instead he sent Ylenia, his faithful secretary. She adjusted her designer glasses on the bridge of her nose. "The Honorable Brianese would like to speak with you," she announced. "But he has a meeting and he won't be able to come by until very late this evening. He begs you to wait for him."

"For Counselor Brianese I'm always available," I replied in the same pompous tone.

She turned to go, stamping her heels ever so slightly. It annoyed her that I hadn't used the term of respect "Honorable" to refer to Brianese, but there was no way I could get the phrase out of my mouth without seeming irreverent.

It was an evening packed with exciting new developments. Martina waved me over to their table and proudly announced that Gemma had decided to quit smoking.

"It's not an easy thing to do," I commented as if she weren't sitting right there. "I know lots of people who tried but couldn't do it."

"Don't be so negative," she scolded me. "You ought to encourage her, not discourage her."

"No, he's right," said the smoker in question, rising to my defense. "But I'm going to do my level best to quit."

Next it was the turn of the proprietor of a well known *enoteca*. He took a seat at the counter and ordered an *amaro*. The bartender reached around to grab the bottle but I stopped him. I pulled out a bottle of cognac from my personal stock and poured a couple of snifters. His eyes were red, with dark circles of anxiety and exhaustion. He was the picture of a man in trouble. It didn't cost me a thing to be nice to him and see if we could be useful to one another.

"I wouldn't expect you to drink a syrupy concoction like that," I said, handing him the snifter.

"I've got problems with my shop and I don't know how to get out of this situation," he muttered in dialect. "Just think, my father started the business as just a humble little wine shop and tavern. Then, when everyone had plenty of money and started putting on airs that they were all wine connoisseurs, and my customers would only drink wine that came out of a bottle with a label and a certification of origin, I changed the sign and took the sommelier course at the Chamber of Commerce . . . "

"And now you're one of the countless businessmen and

shopkeepers hit hard by the downturn, devastated now that the banks have turned off the faucet. You're fifty years old and if you have to shut down your business you don't know how you'll make a living," I summarized in a flat voice so I wouldn't have to listen to the rest of the story of his life. "What can I do for you?"

He rubbed his face with both hands. "I don't want to have to fold my business," he answered with tears in his voice.

"Sorry, I don't make unsecured loans," I told him.

He shook his head and gulped down the cognac. "I'm looking for a partner."

"I'm not interested, I already have my hands full with La Nena," I shot back. Then I pointed to a bundle of paper sticking out of his back pocket. "But I could help you clear out your warehouse."

He unfolded his inventory and laid it flat on the bar. I read through it. First-rate wines and liquor, no question about it. "If I buy it all, what kind of price would you offer?"

He named a figure that was unquestionably fair and advantageous but which I had no intention of paying.

I handed back the inventory. "That's a good price but I can't afford it. Not even on installments."

His eyes were like an open book. "If I don't pay my suppliers soon no one will be willing to supply me with a single bottle of wine on credit."

"Then forget about trying to make money on it. You can't afford to."

He nodded. The new price he named was much more affordable. I managed to clip a little more off the top and we shook hands on it. He turned down my offer of another glassful and walked out of the bar with his head pulled down between his shoulders.

He was just one of many businessmen hunting desperately for a way to keep the family business out of bankruptcy. They were the ones who'd noticed too late that the good times were over and they hadn't run for shelter early enough. More than one of them had wrapped a noose around their neck or run a vacuum cleaner hose from their tailpipe to their car window. The newspapers carried the reports and the politicians even pretended to care. If it weren't for my little ring of whores, La Nena would have dragged me down to the bottom. To keep from winding up like that guy I'd have had to go back to making bank withdrawals with a pistol and a scrawled note. That was just one more reason to make sure that Brianese gave me back my money.

I'd closed out the cash register some time ago and the cooks and waitstaff had already gone home when the Counselor stooped down to enter the restaurant under the half-closed metal roller shutter.

He took a seat on a stool at the bar. "Are we alone?"

"Of course. What are you drinking?"

"Nothing. I'm fine, thanks," he replied before heading off to the back room.

I poured myself a drink and took my time following him back.

"What the fuck did you think you were going to achieve with that bloodbath in my house?" he launched into me, seething with rage.

"Well, this for starters," I replied, continuing my show of tranquility. "An open, honest exchange of ideas. I'm not going to say between friends, but at least between two people who respect one another and behave accordingly."

He smirked. "That's it?"

"Counselor, you never had the slightest intention of paying me back the two million euros you stole from me with the fake scam in Dubai," I started to explain. "You were planning to string me along with just enough bullshit to keep me happy and when the time was up you weren't planning to give me a cent. And you know why?"

"I'm all ears," he replied arrogantly.

"Because you made the mistake of continuing to think of me, with a healthy dose prejudice and contempt, as the man I once was, the man who first came to your office with a bag full of money and a criminal record that needed a good scrubbing."

"Well, what happened, have you changed?" he taunted me.

"That's right. And you're the only one who hasn't noticed."

"You go tell my housekeeper or my wife about your transformation. You turned my home into a nightmare and now you tell me you're an innocent lily of the field?"

"I'm more of one than you are, anyway. And it was the only way I could get your attention."

"You're a sick, dangerous man," he hissed. "In this system nobody does any physical harm to anyone else. You might lose money, which is what happened to you, or you might lose your reputation, or even wind up in jail, but we don't wind up in the hospital or in the boneyard. We're in the Veneto, not in the south of Italy!"

"Then I must just be one of those unpredictable variables in your fucked-up system, Counselor, and I can promise you that I've shown considerable restraint and offered no more than a tiny demonstration of the extent of my professional skills in the field of inflicting violence. You can't even begin to imagine how good I am at the work I do . . . "

He turned white as a sheet, but his tone betrayed no fear. "Don't you dare threaten me."

"I wouldn't dream of it. Otherwise I'd be sitting here with a lengthy list of demands," I shot back. "I want just one thing: from now on you are going to have to respect the obligations you've undertaken with me."

"Is that all?"

"Two million euros, plus 25 percent interest, within a year."

He stood there in silence and stared at me for a while, then he turned on his heel and headed for the door.

"Counselor," I called after him in a loud, cutting voice. "The Nena, as always, is at your service, but it's not free anymore."

"That's fine," he said, as he wrapped his cashmere scarf around his neck in a loose knot. "I'll have Ylenia get in touch with you. She takes care of all those details."

"Go fuck yourself, asshole," I muttered through clenched teeth. I sat there enjoying my cognac in the silence of the back room. I had created that room so that he'd feel secure as he negotiated deals and laid traps for his enemies.

Instead, the smart thing would have been to salt the place with microphones. As I came and went with plates and bottles I'd overheard snatches of conversation that, offered for sale in a tidy package, would have allowed me to triple the sum the Counselor owed me now.

The toxic leachings from a dump poured into the open sea in order to reduce waste disposal costs, bribes paid to tamper with the health department statistics on tumors caused by an incinerator, more bribes to persuade world-renowned university professors to express support for nuclear- and coal-powered electricity, defective but inexpensive prosthetic limbs and hip replacements, which would later have to be replaced at the price of two operations instead of one, engineering studies designed to ensure that two absolutely useless highway bypasses . . .

I remember once having to separate two furious engineers, each of them the director of a respected planning firm, who were trading punches over some deal involved in the design for a new hospital.

I'd been an idiot. Instead of playing dirty with Brianese, I'd protected him, coddled him, even served as his bootlicking pimp with the sole objective of winning the honor of his respect and his patronage of La Nena.

And how did he repay me? By conning me out of two million euros.

I shut the place down and went home to Martina and her creams and ointments.

The next morning my wife talked at length about Gemma and her efforts at self-improvement. The more she talked about her friend the more uneasy I felt. There was no way I was going to be able to restrain myself. The only thing left was to figure when and how I was going to cross that line.

I changed the subject. "How is your father?"

"No better. It's inconceivable to me that modern science can't come up with a cure for it."

I looked up from the jar of yogurt that my cook made for me. "And it seems inconceivable to me that you should utter such claptrap."

She stuck her tongue out at me while she added a spoonful of cane sugar to her mug of tea. "I thought I'd spend three mornings with him, Monday, Wednesday, and Friday, and I'll reschedule my Zumba Fitness, Pilates, and Gliding Disc classes for the afternoons, along with my massages and my jogging."

"That's too many things clustered together," I commented as I glanced over at the sheet of paper with her weekly schedule hanging on the refrigerator. "Your body can't take it all. You're going to have to give up running."

She looked at me in surprise. She hadn't seen that one coming. "I can tweak your diet, but there aren't any other solutions," I added. "Obviously, you'll have to give up alcohol entirely, because that sly dog just turns into a nasty yellowish fat that you can never get rid of."

"But I hardly drink anything!"

"So it won't be a sacrifice to give it up completely."

I smooched and cuddled with her for a couple of minutes. "Now I really have to go."

"I wish we could just go on a holiday somewhere together. Just the two of us, alone on a dreamy beach . . . "

I shuddered at the thought as memories of our honeymoon in Polynesia came back to me. "When La Nena is running smoothly enough for me to leave," I said offhandedly, as I opened the door. I paused but there was no need for me to turn around to make my meaning clear. "This is a tough period and the last thing on my mind is a vacation."

Ylenia was waiting for me, consoling herself with a cappuccino and rice cake. I ordered a glass of Alpine chamois milk for myself, La Nena's newest breakfast offering.

"I've drawn up a prospectus with the various initiatives and a preliminary estimate of costs as a basis for discussion," she began her pitch, opening an elegant leather portfolio. "We expect you to make a special effort with favorable prices, as a personal contribution to the political battle we're about to undertake to defend the position of the party here in the region."

I looked at her. She was attractive in spite of the severe cut of her suit, her flat heels, her smooth shoulder-length hair. Her body was petite but shapely, her features were slightly angular but agreeable. Her legs were her weak spot, with oversized ankles and calves.

She returned my look with an arrogant glance and at that very moment, for no exact reason, I felt sure that she and Brianese were lovers. I'd considered that possibility before but I'd dismissed it. I'd never assigned much importance to that young woman in her early thirties, always impeccable but never spectacular. I'd written her off as "the secretary that any professional would want": presentable and efficient.

And once again I'd been wrong. The many years of difference in their ages had done nothing to prevent her from having a relationship with the Counselor, the famous lawyer, the man who never lost a case, who'd gone into politics and was becoming increasingly famous and powerful. And corrupt. I wondered how much she knew about his business dealings. If he was just taking her to bed then maybe not much, but if the two of them were really in love then she was his accomplice and his confidante.

Ylenia interpreted my silence as an invitation to go on with a presentation of their political objectives.

"There's no need for you to talk me into it," I interrupted. "Let me have that prospectus."

I was afraid that I was going to have to endure prolonged negotiations, but the prices set out in the prospectus were quite reasonable. "These aren't the kind of prices that I was expecting," I lied. "But given my many years of friendship with Counselor Brianese and in view of the contributions that we must all make to the party, I'm going to accept them without discussion."

I saw a smirk of contempt play across her lips that I didn't like one bit. I asked her to sit and chat a little longer, and to call me by my first name. I unleashed the full force of my personal charm, but to no avail. She put away her papers and stood up. She held out her hand, nicely manicured and adorned with at least 20,000 euros' worth of rings.

"Arrivederci," she said, without meeting my glance.

That bitch knows a lot more than she ought to, I mused. My instincts as a former guerrilla warrior and an ex-armed robber had saved my ass on more than one occasion, and now they were warning me to be wary of Ylenia. She suddenly looked like she could be a dangerous adversary or, even worse, a loose cannon. I felt like kicking myself for the idiot that I'd been. I'd known her since the day Brianese hired her, and I'd never noticed a thing.

I quickly got rid of a sales representative touting French cheeses and told the senior waiter that I was going to be away for a while.

Roby De Palma was an assiduous customer of La Nena and

many other clubs, bars, and restaurants frequented by people with money. He was a private investigator, and being well known was the best way to get jobs. He mostly did small-time investigations, and I used him to check out my employees. Both when I hired them and afterward, with periodic checkups. I wasn't interested in running the risk of finding out too late that one bad apple had fucked up the reputation of my establishment. Roby was no genius, but the good thing about him was that he knew the right people and he managed to lay his hands on information that was completely confidential.

I hopped into a taxi and rode over to his office, in a big nondescript building in the industrial district, now almost entirely occupied by Chinese import-export companies.

When he ushered me into his office he pointed to the *Gazzetta dello Sport* lying open on his desk. "I was just going over an important case," he joked.

I sat down on the office chair. "Ylenia Mazzonetto."

"Brianese's secretary?"

"That's right."

"What do you want to know?"

"Anything she doesn't want people to know."

"You're not going to get me into trouble, are you?"

"Don't worry. I think she's hot and I'm curious about her."

"You think she's hot? Come on, don't bullshit me! She's cute, but there are so many choice pieces of ass at your restaurant . . . "

I shrugged. "I've got a lot of money on the line in this upcoming election and she's managing it all . . . "

"That's better," he responded. "But do you have enough money for me? This is the kind of investigation that can drag out."

"Don't take advantage," I warned him. "Most of all, don't think of handing over 'my information' to the Padanos. I know you've crossed over . . . "

He made a show of taking offense. "Who do you take me for? You know I have solid professional ethics."

He counted the bills in the envelope that I'd handed him. "Let's say, twice this amount, agreed?"

"Sure, when you've completed a first-class investigation," I replied as I got to my feet.

"You should think about joining us," he said as he walked me to the door. "The Padanos are the future, here."

I extended my arms helplessly. "I've been joined at the hip with Brianese for far too long and La Nena is going to be his reception space during the election campaign . . . It's too late to change course now."

"It's not like you'd have to have a membership card . . . " he commented. "Shit, I remember when my dad used to carry four or five party membership cards: Christian Democratic Party, Italian Socialist Party, and even the Italian Social-Democratic Party, whatever the hell that ever was."

"I'll think it over," I lied.

At the end of a dull day the Honorable Brianese came in to drink an aperitif, accompanied by Ylenia and Nicola. He behaved the way he usually did and was especially affectionate and courteous with me. He sang my praises so that everyone could hear and announced that La Nena would be a major venue for the party's campaign events.

"If you want to tip back a glass in the company of major figures of the Italian political landscape, you'll have to come here."

Then he waved me over. "You can open the back room up again," he said in a hushed voice. "The establishment is now a public place and there are going to be plenty of journalists in here. We can't afford to run any risks. A smart reporter can put two and two together in a flash."

I smelled a rat. "What about my girls: they're still available to you, right?"

"Maybe before the elections we'd all better try to be good boys. I think not until afterwards . . . "

The Counselor stood up, apologized but said that he couldn't stay for dinner, and then left with his trusted colleagues. I noticed Roby De Palma down his spritz in a gulp and then discreetly follow the trio.

With one deft and technically impeccable move Brianese had cut me off from all access to the important circles. With the excuse that he didn't want to be seen in the company of individuals who might arouse the curiosity of professional busybodies, he succeeded in preventing future conversations like the one that had allowed me to discover through Domenico Beccaro the way he'd cheated me on the Dubai scam. But it didn't make any sense that he no longer wanted to make use of my service for his supply of pretty girls. Nobody else but me could reliably protect him and his friends from gossip and scandals, and there was no question of any of them being able to keep their dicks in their pants through an entire election campaign.

I had to pretend that I was happy about the designation of my establishment, but I was actually seething with rage. The Counselor went on relentlessly mocking me. I forced myself to make my usual round of the tables with a smile on my lips.

"So Gemma, are you withstanding the temptation to light a cigarette?" I asked when I got to the table where she was having dinner with Martina.

"Certainly," she answered proudly.

"Just think, she's even given up her usual aperitif tonight, to stand by me in my new alcohol-free regimen," my wife broke in.

I looked at her in surprise. "Good girl!" Then I turned to my wife: "Do you think she's finally made up her mind to find herself a man?"

Gemma blushed. I gave her a paternal pinch on the cheek and moved on to another table.

I thought about Martina, about saying to her: "Spinning,

baby, spinning," and the peace and quiet that would come next, when I'd finally have a chance to think clearly.

A little before closing time De Palma came back. "The secretary Ylenia is screwing the Honorable Brianese," he announced. "You know those residential hotels, designed for discretion, where you park in the underground structure and use the elevator to get upstairs?"

He waited for me to nod in agreement before continuing. "This one's outside of town and the apartment's in the name of a company, Nasco Costruzioni SpA, that officially uses it as accommodations for the structural engineers that come in from out of town."

"How did you manage to find out all this information at this time of night?"

He pulled his cell phone out of the pocket of his down jacket. "A phone call to the right person."

The two partners who owned Nasco had attended a number of dinner parties in the back room with Brianese and enjoyed the charms of my girls. But I was careful not to tell that to the private investigator.

"I want to know if you're asking me to keep pursuing this trail," he asked me.

"Why do you ask?"

"Because I'd prefer to know exactly what you're looking for, rather than running the risk of finding out things I really don't want to be involved in. I can smell a distinctive aroma of shit and of politics too, but I can't say which of the two smells is stronger."

"You've been frank and I want to be just as clear. I want to know exactly how many hairs there are on the ass of Signorina Ylenia Mazzonetto, and if you happen to find out anything else, I'm ready and willing to pay the difference."

"There's no need. You're a good client and this is a nice place with good food and good drink."

He sketched out something like a military salute and turned to go.

So I'd seen clearly: Brianese and Ylenia were in a relationship and I found out late. Doing my best to be an upright and honest citizen for eleven years had made me blind, foolish, and defenseless. The Counselor had figured that out and decided that I deserved to be ripped off to the tune of two million euros. I had reacted and he'd been forced to adopt a counter-strategy to keep me on ice, but the message was unmistakable: he was still and would always remain the stronger one.

I was deeply uninterested in trying to see whose dick was longer. My only objective was to get my hands onto the 2.25 million euros that he owed me.

Time seemed to stand still. I needed Martina and the incessant swishing of the freewheel of the spinner bike. I locked up the bar and was walking briskly home when I happened to cross paths with three girls out strolling, carefree, chatting and smoking. I changed direction.

"I wasn't expecting you," said Gemma in a voice that quavered slightly.

I extended my foot inside the door and then withdrew it quickly. "I can come in or I can pretend I was never here. What should I do?"

She swallowed. "You can come in, if you want."

I did the same thing with my foot, but very slowly this time. "This game has different rules: I'll come in only if you ask me. I promise you, though, if I come in, nothing will ever be the same."

"Are you trying to scare me?"

"I just want you to be well aware of what's going to happen," I murmured. "I'm the Big Bad Wolf, and I gobble up Little Red Riding Hood and then I take the grandmother and the hunter and I fuck them both in the ass."

She closed her eyes to enjoy the shiver that was running up and down her back. "Come in."

I left the apartment a few hours later. Gemma, nude and drunk, was smoking and crying, curled up on a sofa.

My wife was on the sofa too. She must have waited up for me and then fallen asleep. On the large and expensive plasma screen scenes from an old television series were flowing past. I went to take a shower to get the smell of Gemma off me.

"Sorry if I fell asleep," Martina apologized the next morning as she poured my coffee. "You must have come home late and I didn't hear you."

I said nothing. I just looked at her. Actually I was thinking about something else, and specifically I was musing that I couldn't believe that Brianese would take the risk of making use of a network of women of easy virtue without a corresponding certificate guaranteeing total discretion. He had too much at risk and for the most part his business partners were individuals of the stature of Domenico Beccaro, ready to engage in foolish and reckless behavior with women very different from the ones they'd married, and then brag about it like little boys. My beautiful girls, in contrast, were fleeting apparitions between silk sheets in the beds of unfamiliar villas, and even if cops and investigating magistrates focused on reconstructing dates, locations, and situations, they wouldn't be able to lay their hands on anything solid.

As far as I knew, there were no organizations capable of offering that same level of security. The only possible explanation was that Brianese himself had assigned one of his clients to take care of it, and suggested the proper methods and procedures.

I grabbed Martina by the shoulders. "I'm expecting you to come up with something appropriate tonight."

She heaved a sigh of relief. "Of course, darling. Tell me how you'd like me to . . . "

I raised my voice slightly. "Maybe for once you could make the effort and use a little imagination, what do you think?"

Nicoletta arranged to meet me in a shopping mall in a neighboring province where she had paid a call on a woman she worked for. She had the Chinese girl with her. She'd named her Lin. She'd given the same name to all the Chinese girls she'd managed before this one. They were all the same to her.

"Go look at some shop windows," I ordered Lin.

"Are you in a bad mood? Is there some problem?" my partner asked.

"Brianese has cut us off. At least until after the elections."

"Is there a reason?"

"He said he doesn't want to run risks."

"Bullshit," she snarled. "During election campaigns all of them fuck like rabbits. Orgies, betrayals, new alliances, expressions of gratitude. You name it, it's an occasion for sex . . . "

"Well, whatever the reason, we're out. We need to make a decision."

"Shutting down the operation makes no sense," Nicoletta shot back with determination. "We have the girls, the houses, we know how to do this . . . it'll be tough at first but in a few months we can put together a nice network of customers."

"What kind of network?" I asked. "There'll never be enough of a critical mass just working with foreign businessmen and I can't send you people from La Nena or even spread the word. That's the easiest way to wind up in jail."

"I've made investments and I can't risk losing everything."

"Neither can I," I said to myself, thinking of La Nena. "In a little while time's up for this group of girls," I announced. "And while on the one hand we're technically in the black because we sell them for twice what we paid for them, on the other hand we have to dress them, train them . . . I don't think it's worth it."

"I agree. I think we need to hold onto these four until we can get through the crisis." She could see I was skeptical. "Trust me. I have these girls living in a world of cocks, lingerie, reality shows, and South American and Chinese soap operas. They don't know anything dangerous."

I wasn't completely convinced, but maybe it was worth giving it a try for a few months; after all, in terms of sales we wouldn't be losing anything.

"All right," I snorted with some exasperation. "Keep me posted. I'll take a look around and see if we can find a politician to take Brianese's place, though I don't have very high hopes."

As I headed back into the center of town I did some rough calculations. With the revenue from the election campaign I'd be able to cut La Nena's losses considerably, but I'd still have to put a little of my own money into it to close the books without a loss, and the whores weren't bringing in the money that they used to. It was a mess. My future increasingly hung from the money that Brianese had promised to pay me back.

Three days later, Roby De Palma showed up at lunchtime. "Do you have a minute to drop by my office this afternoon?"

"Today we're serving pasta fagioli and baccalà alla vicentina, accompanied by a spectacular red Tokaj," I tempted him. "If you want, pick a table and we can chat after you have dessert."

He pointed to a couple that was enjoying an antipasto made of shredded air-dried horsemeat. "I'll sit over there. The man is a dentist and I need a couple of cavities filled . . . "

Martina was tired. She'd taken care of her father all morning. I took pity on her and told the waiter to bring her a slice of *pinza*, a pastry dating back to the earliest Venetian tradition, made of cornmeal and dried fruit. She blew me a kiss from the table.

At 2:30 on the dot the kitchen closed, and latecomers had to settle for sandwiches and cold dishes. Roby De Palma was sipping his second grappa when I waved to him to join me in the back room.

"I've never been in here," he said.

"It used to be a private space, for corporate clients only, but now I'm making it available to all my clients. Even the biggest companies are trying to save money these days."

The private investigator booted up a laptop. "After we're done I'll give you a flash drive with the report and the pictures."

I sat down beside him. "Did you find what I'm looking for?"

"I couldn't say," he said. "I just know I'm not taking this any further."

"You must have your good reasons."

"I don't want to make any enemies," he said. "In this line of work, I can make a very nice living if I stick to the lower levels, if you know what I mean."

"I understand perfectly."

"Should I start from the day she was born or should I skip the preliminaries?"

"Get straight to the point, Roby."

He clicked on a folder containing photographs and started scrolling through them. Each picture had a date and location. "Our fair Ylenia doesn't go with Brianese to Rome but she's never in the office either," he started to narrate the images. "She meets plenty of people all over the Veneto, most of them in the light of day . . . "

"She's drumming up votes for her boss."

"Sure. But sometimes she acts a little funny," he added in an ironic tone of voice. "She meets people in odd places, like at gymnasiums, department stores, parking structures . . . Now do you understand why I'd just as soon bring this investigation to a close?"

I was about to answer him when I suddenly recognized a person who was talking with Ylenia in the coffee shop of a major bookstore outside of Treviso; my blood ran cold when I checked the date.

"That woman's been a regular in your restaurant for years," the private investigator commented.

"She's the only one who has nothing to do with the alleged business dealings of Brianese and Mazzonetto," I lied, doing my best to be persuasive. "Nicoletta Rizzardi sells lingerie to all the women she knows. She supplies my wife regularly as well. They meet after her Pilates class."

I had the impression he'd taken me at my word. He showed me a few more photographs, which I looked at without paying any attention at all, then he turned off his computer. "When do I get paid?" he asked in a flat, pragmatic tone of voice.

"Come by tonight, I'll buy you an aperitif."

I walked him to the door and then returned to my post at the cash register. Good old Nicoletta! Even my business partner had decided to screw me. I'd been racking my brains trying to figure out who was supplying Brianese with call girls that met my security standards and all along it had been me. I'd even let them take my whores away from me. By now it was clear that the Counselor had laid out a strategy to ensure that I could no longer do him any harm while he enjoyed the benefits of my money, or perhaps to ruin me, or worse, to destroy me.

Then and there I felt like going to see Nicoletta, load her into my car along with the other girls, and pay a call on the Maltese gangsters. I'd be rid of her for good, just like all the other girls that we'd managed and dispatched to our various clients as call girls. But that would have been a mistake. Another in a long succession of mistakes. The time had come to remember who I once was, what I'd done to get ahead.

I'd shot my best friend in the head, I'd betrayed, cheated, raped, robbed, and eliminated anyone who got in the way of my reaching my objective.

They'd all known a different man, a man who was willing to do anything to please people and to be accepted. None of them had even the slightest idea of who Giorgio Pellegrini really was.

Chapter Two
King of Hearts

I spent a little time verifying Nicoletta's betrayal. It didn't take much: all I had to do was keep an eye on the villas. I eliminated all doubt the day I saw Brianese step out of a Porsche Panamera along with two members of the provincial administration and a well-known face from local television, only to be greeted at the door by my partner.

Evidently, everything they were already doing was not enough to make me "innocuous." The final blow was still looming, and it was driving me crazy that I couldn't figure out what kind of plan the Counselor had come up with. Luckily the election campaign had begun and La Nena was draining all my energy. It was only at closing time that my mind overflowed with thoughts and nightmares that I was forced to take out on Martina and Gemma. I tended to protect my wife, even though she was ready and willing to immolate herself with love and devotion. I took out the brunt of it on her best friend.

One night, while I was getting my clothes back on, Gemma stood up and staggered over to the stereo. A second later the voice of Caterina Caselli came out of the speakers:

You think you're the King of Hearts
And you grab a heart whenever you like
You keep it for a while
Close to you
But then you drop it . . .

"Turn that off," I snapped in annoyance.

"No, no . . . listen to the words . . . "

The bitter north wind
Breaks off flowers here and there
You break the heart
Of a girl who's no more than a child
A heart you hold in your hand.
Life is a river
Sweeping you down . . .
King of Hearts,
I'd like to know
Where your heart might be . . .

I hit the "off" switch. Caselli's voice reminded me of another song that I thought I'd erased from my memory. Roberta liked *I'll Never See You Again*, and it had become our song. At her funeral, I'd had them write on the wreath "Arrivederci amore, ciao." It was our goodbye kiss.

Gemma went on, half-humming half-singing the chorus: "King of Hearts, I'd like to know where your heart might be," and pointing her index finger at me.

I grabbed her by the chin. "Shut up."

"You're the King of Hearts, I know it."

"Don't talk bullshit."

"Just like I know that you killed Roberta."

I grabbed her by the hair and forced her to her knees on the floor. "I understand your little game and I don't like it one bit."

"She was no good for you, she didn't understand that the only way to love you is to abandon yourself and plunge down into the abyss that you dig for every woman that lets you get near her."

I shoved her to the floor and I put on my pants. Gemma slithered along the floor to my legs and grabbed them tight.

"Listen, I'm begging you, I don't care about Roberta. I only want you to know that you can do whatever you like with me."

"You're nothing but a pastime for me, Gemma," I said, prodding her. "Martina is and will always be the only woman in my life."

"Pastime, plaything, doll, toy, diversion, amusement . . . I'm anything you want me to be, King of Hearts, as long as you use me."

"Look at me."

I stared at her for a long time and what I saw in her eyes triggered a wave of desire inside me. I shoved her into the kitchen and when she understood what I had in mind she started chuckling softly.

"This is going to drive me crazy, King of Hearts."

I went home a little after nine in the morning. Martina was sitting in a chair close to the front door. She leapt to her feet with tears in her eyes. "Oh, Giorgio, I was so worried."

I didn't say a single word. She helped me off with my overcoat as she chattered away about what a horribly hellish night she'd just spent. When she laid her head on my chest she caught the whiff of another woman. She stiffened and went to move away from me but I held her tight. She tried to break free but I was too strong.

"Why would you do this to me, Giorgio?" she sobbed.

"Because I love you."

"You know that you don't need any other women but me."

"This is a tough period. But we'll get through it if you stand by me and prove that you love me."

"It's hard to accept that I'm not the only one anymore."

"Try to be strong."

She wept for a few minutes. "I hope I don't know her," she said, blowing her nose. "She uses the same perfume as Gemma, but so do lots of women."

"Draw me a bath."

While Martina was scrubbing my legs with the bath sponge I decided that the time had come to have a conversation with Mikhail.

I met him in the usual service plaza outside Bologna. I played the part of his sidekick in the same old skit about him sharing a last name with the Soviet writer Sholokhov, but when he pulled out his laptop to show me the new catalogue of girls he was importing, I explained the real reason I'd asked him to come to that meeting.

He thought about my proposal for a few minutes, giving me a mistrustful glance every so often. "It's an unusual request," he commented. "But it's also true that we're talking about a lot of money."

"Then what's the problem?"

"You're the problem," he replied. "You see, I have a long history of getting ripped off, which is why I'm satisfied with collecting the money from the tricks turned by a crew of prostitutes, beating them up without leaving marks when they misbehave, and taking orders from a couple of wicked witches, who pay off a deputy commissioner of police every month to the tune of twenty-five thousand euros so he'll keep the cops out of the picture . . . "

"Excuse me, Mikhail, but I have no idea what you're driving at. You make side deals with me and you screw your two employers in the process."

He sighed in exasperation. "It's never any fun to talk with you northern Italians . . . you can never complete a thought the way you'd like."

I stretched out my arms helplessly. "I'm sorry, go on with what you were saying . . . "

"I know plenty of criminals like you. As long as we're talking about you giving me money for girls, everything's fine, but if the work involves violence, you're one of those guys that in the end winds up killing his partner so he doesn't have to split the take. Do you see what I'm talking about?"

I stared at him open-mouthed, but then I burst into a hearty belly laugh.

"You're right, Mikhail. That's exactly how I am. But in this case, there's no take to split. If you like, I'll pay you for the job in advance."

"Then I'll do it."

I spent twenty minutes or so explaining the plan in detail and answering his questions.

"You speak Italian very well, Mikhail," I said after we were done.

"Even though I'm a Cossack?" he joked, careful not to rise to the bait. But I was no fool either and I could detect a university education, even in a fellow pimp.

On my way back to work I drove past Nicoletta's house and when I noticed her car parked out front I decided to pay an unannounced visit. She opened the door with a cigarette dangling from her lips and pretended she was happy to see me.

"Anything wrong?" she asked.

"No. I was just in the neighborhood and I figured I'd drop by and talk about our situation."

On the living room table a computer was humming and papers were scattered everywhere. "I'm trying to get my accounting into some kind of order," she explained.

"Tell me about it. I just leave it all to my CPA these days."

Nicoletta asked me in and offered me something to drink.

"The girls?" I asked.

She pointed upstairs. "They're resting."

I flashed a contented smile. "Then a little bit of work is coming in after all, now and then."

"Don't get your hopes up. It was four drunk Danes we found at the Venice Casino."

I looked out the window. Through the blinds I could see lots of other little villas, all the same. "I'm really busy with La Nena, these days. I very much doubt that I can find time to help you drum up clients," I said in a forlorn tone.

She reached out and grabbed my arm. "Don't worry. I'll take care of it myself."

I stood up. "If you change your mind and you want to sell the whole package I only need two day's notice."

She nodded. "Let's see how things turn out after the elections."

I gave her a kiss on the cheek and left. I'd officially started the dance and for the first time my mind was at peace. In the afternoon there was a brief cocktail party for the Minister of Defense, but it would last no more than half an hour.

I called Martina. "What's playing at the theater tonight?"

Then I called Gemma. "Ciao, King of Hearts," she greeted me.

"In a few minutes Martina is going to call you," I warned her. "This evening you're coming to the theater with us. Do your best to be a good girl."

I behaved like a perfect gentleman. Martina began to relax and once we were back home I rubbed the creams into her skin, and then I carried her in my arms to our bed, where we made love with ecstatic tenderness.

The next morning I woke up to the happiest woman in the world.

I spun Gemma a story about how that week would be hellishly busy at La Nena and that she shouldn't expect to see much of me. I only went over once and I only stayed a couple of hours. I enjoyed peppering her with intimate questions. She was embarrassed and reticent.

I pointed to the door. "I can always leave."

She shook her head. I left her drained and sucked dry. Disoriented. I knew the feeling all too well. I'd learned the technique from a DIGOS cop called Anedda who had transformed me into a turncoat and a puppet.

At the end of a dull day during which, from the morning on, there was one campaign event after another and I'd even had the honor of being photographed with my arms wrapped around a couple of showgirls, my cell phone rang. When I read the name on the display I heaved a sigh of relief.

"Something horrible's happened," Nicoletta shouted in a panicky voice. "Get over to my house immediately."

"Calm down and tell me what . . . "

"I can't, goddamn it! And Jesus, hurry, please, hurry. I don't know what to do!"

I hung up with a big smile on my face. At last Mikhail had gone into action. I poured myself a couple of fingers of cognac to celebrate the new development and I struck up a conversation with an official at a certain local agency who'd been frequenting the establishment for a while with an unmistakable look on his face that spelled out the words: I can be bribed.

I took my time getting there and when my partner opened the door to my knock she was in a state of complete meltdown. "Jesus, Giorgio, what took you so long?" she mumbled.

In the living room I found Isabel stretched out on the sofa, moaning, holding a bloodsoaked towel against the right side of her face. Along the edge of the towel was printed the name of a hotel in Chioggia.

"What the hell happened?" I asked.

"Some crazy Russian disfigured her face," Nicoletta replied, revealing the Venezuelan girl's damaged features.

"Wow, talk about disfigured," I replied, looking at the open cut that ran from her jaw to well beyond her chin. "He completely ruined her."

"I don't know what to do, Giorgio."

"The first thing to do is get a clean towel and some ice, then see if you can find some painkillers."

I slipped on a pair of latex gloves that I just happened to have in my pocket and I examined the wound a little more carefully. Mikhail had asked what kind of a cut I preferred.

"Jagged-edged, like the cut a carefully sharpened metal comb would make," I replied.

"Like that cut-up whore in the movie with Clint Eastwood and Gene Hackman. I think it was called *Unforgiven*."

"Exactly, that's how I want her: completely useless in terms of ever working again."

The Russian had been a man of his word. My partner came back with the things I'd requested. I put a couple of tablets in the girl's mouth and made her swallow them with a hefty slug of rum. Then I wrapped the towel around the ice and put it against the wound.

"Hold it like that, good girl."

"Why aren't you taking me to the hospital?" Isabel said rebelliously.

"Just be patient for a few minutes," I replied, grabbing the liquor bottle.

Halfway through the third glass she passed out.

"At last!" Nicoletta blurted. "I don't know how much longer I could have listened to that whore whining."

Her hands were shaking and she couldn't get her lighter to work. I took it out of her hand and helped her to light her cigarette.

"Relax and tell me everything."

Nicoletta paid a night clerk at a hotel to find her customers for her girls. That night a distinguished Russian gentleman had taken a room and asked for an "extra blanket" for the whole night. He'd made it clear that money was no object. She'd brought Isabel around after dinner and the Russian had fucked her to a fare-thee-well. But then he'd started playing around with certain objects and the girl had raised objections. The Russian didn't like that and he'd cut her face.

"And then?"

"The Russian left and the night clerk called me and told me to get Isabel out of there while he cleaned up the room."

"Where are the other girls?"

She turned pale. They were in bed with friends of Brianese but she certainly couldn't tell me that. "They're with other clients," she lied.

"What other clients?" I asked.

"What the hell do you care?" she shouted. "Can't you see what a mess we're in?"

I spoke to her in a calm tone of voice. "I was only trying to figure out if we have enough time left to try to hush this whole thing up."

"They're at the villa outside of Vicenza. I can tell them to spend the night there and go pick them up in the morning." Then she pointed to Isabel slumped over on the couch. "So what do we do now?"

I ran a hand over my face, pretending I was trying to think. "One thing's for sure: we can't take her to the hospital looking like this. Two minutes later the police would be questioning us."

I took the towel off the Venezuelan girl's face. "What we need is a good plastic surgeon and a proper operating room to fix this disaster," I pointed out to her. "It's just too bad we're not in business with Brianese anymore. He'd know the right people and a couple of phone calls from him would keep the cops off our backs."

Nicoletta gave me a sharp glance, uncertain whether she should tell me the truth and hand over her betrayal on a silver platter. As I expected, though, she decided not to say a word. Which gave me the chance to lead her into my trap.

"No matter what we do, she's not worth shit on the market

anymore," I said. "We'd be stuck with her, along with a lovely pink scar and a burning desire for vengeance."

"What are you trying to say?"

"What do you think's going to happen when she wakes up lying on that sofa instead of in a hospital bed? She won't be the naïve little fool you've been steering around up till now. She'll turn into an angry woman with nothing to lose, willing to do anything to keep from being an unsightly monster for the rest of her life."

Nicoletta broke down. She turned on the waterworks and started sobbing. "So what the fuck are we supposed to do now?"

"We just eliminate the problem," I responded seraphically.

She leapt to her feet. "Are you fucking insane?" she screamed.

I put on my overcoat and neatly tucked my scarf into place while my partner howled like a banshee. With that hoarse voice of hers she really was hard to take. I waved goodbye and headed for the door.

She grabbed me by the half-belt on the back of my coat to keep me from leaving. "Where do you think you're going, asshole?"

I gave her a smack. I followed it up with another. "I'm going home to get some sleep because I'm beat and I've worked hard all day," I told her. "And you're taking your whore to the emergency room and then you're going to have some explaining to do to the cops because she's going to tell them about the hotel and the Russian with the knife, and how you loaded her into your car and left the hotel without calling an ambulance or the police. Plus, to save his ass, the night clerk is going to tell them all about how you bribed him to let you run hookers out of his hotel. And then they'll work their way back to the other three. Should I go on?"

She shook her head and slumped into an armchair and started to whimper again. "Unless you have a better idea . . . "

I added. "But if you can't think of anything . . . well then, I don't see how else we can settle the matter."

"I could let you take care of it."

"Gladly."

I unwrapped the expensive silk scarf from around her neck and ran it around Isabel's throat. I braced one knee against her spine and started tugging. She was dead in less than a minute.

Nicoletta was frozen with shock. She jammed both her hands, balled into fists, against her mouth and stood staring at the girl's dead body. "You just killed her."

"And I did it with your silk scarf," I pointed out, using the scarf to secure the towel around the dead girl's face.

"Now what are you doing?"

"You wouldn't want to get blood all over your car."

I made her give me the keys to her SUV, I slung Isabel over my shoulder, and I dumped her into the ample luggage space in back.

Before going out the door I called the Russian. "I'm on my way, with my friend."

Mikhail was waiting for me in a dark country lane. I pulled up twenty minutes later, after a roundabout drive through empty parts of town.

"I've already got the hole dug," he told me.

I noticed his hand gripping a handgun pointing at the ground.

"You really don't trust me, do you?"

"You know how these things go, my friend. This is exactly when they decide to kill you and you wind up at the bottom of the grave you just dug, keeping a corpse company. Then the next thing you know a hotel night clerk has identified both dead bodies and the police close the books on a turbulent love affair gone wrong."

"I wish I'd thought of that myself," I kidded him, as I swung open the back hatch of the SUV.

Nicoletta had regained a modicum of self-control. With a cigarette dangling from her lips she was packing up the personal effects of the unfortunate Isabel in her upstairs bedroom. I saw a roll of bills on the night table. I tucked the cash into my overcoat pocket.

"She won't be needing it."

"Where did you . . . "

"Do you really want to know?"

She shook her head and cigarette ashes tumbled onto the clothing piled on the bed. "What should I tell the other girls?"

"The same fairytale that they're all wishing would come true," I answered. "The Russian fell in love with her, bought her from you, and took her off to Moscow to live a life of luxury surrounded by sable stoles, caviar, vodka, and diamonds."

"That's such a moronic story they'd probably fall for it."

I watched her pack for a while. "I think you should listen to me very carefully right now, Nicoletta. I wouldn't want for there to be anything less than a perfect understanding between the two of us."

"What are you talking about?"

"A series of small but meaningful details," I replied. "Buried along with Isabel, who is very well protected by a plastic bag, is your silk scarf and one of your own personal towels, along with the towel from the hotel."

"Why are you threatening me? You know I'll never talk."

"See what I mean? You're still not listening carefully, the way I asked you to," I scolded her. "I'm telling you that everything surrounding this murder points straight at you and only you."

I held out my hands, encased in latex gloves.

"I didn't leave my fingerprints on anything, but you did. There's blood in your nice living room and in your SUV, and there's no way you'll be able to eliminate every last trace of it."

"But you killed her."

"Maybe so, but the evidence all points to you," I explained in a faintly whiny, pedantic tone of voice. "I want to remind you that the night clerk saw you take a bleeding Isabel away from the hotel. And that's something any criminal court in the country would view as a decisive piece of testimony," I added as I held up a clear pastic bag holding the bottle of rum that I'd made sure to pick up before walking upstairs.

"And here are your fingerprints on this bottle, along with the dead girl's."

"You bastard," she hissed, as she lunged for the bag. I rammed my fist into her solar plexus. It wasn't a hard punch, but it stopped her cold.

"Why are you doing this to me?"

"I trust you, Nicoletta. We've been friends for a long time, we're business partners, and I wouldn't give up your blowjobs for anything in the world—they're definitely the best in town. But people change and so I'd like to be positive that you would never try to rip me off."

I blew her a kiss and slipped out of the house, walking through the dark to the car I'd parked in a nearby street.

I watched Martina applying her creams and thought back to Isabel. It had been eleven years since the last time I killed somebody. Back then, I'd sworn to myself that I'd never do it again, because I believed that I'd never need to eliminate stumbling blocks along my straight and narrow path to a normal life. Turns out, I was wrong, but that wasn't my fault.

When Martina reached her orgasm I reflected on the fact that it hadn't been unpleasant at all.

The Nicoletta Rizzardi who walked into La Nena the following day was a very different woman from the one I first met. Her brash, tough attitude, the assumption that she could keep any man in line, had been replaced by the certain knowledge that she was in a situation with no way out and her future dangled by the very thin thread of my benevolence. For the first time, she had no silk scarf around her neck.

I told the waitress to set a table for two in the back room. The second seating for lunch was drawing to a close, and once I was done ringing up the checks I joined her. I was gleefully cruel.

"I expect love from you, Nicoletta. Lots of love." I started the conversation in a syrupy voice.

Her eyes widened. "Love?"

"Have I or have I not become the single most important man in your life?"

"I'm afraid you have."

"Then you're going to have to love me, or at least you're going to have to do such a good job of pretending to love me that I can't tell the difference."

"Stop it, Giorgio, please."

I changed my tone of voice. "Do you think I'm joking?"

She stared at me. "Not for a second."

A waitress walked in with our bowls of pasta. I was hungry and I greedily dug in to the *tagliatelle con ragù di sorana dei colli Berici*. But my partner didn't seem to have much of an appetite.

"How'd it go with the girls?" I asked, wiping the sauce off the bottom of the bowl with a hunk of bread.

"Fine. They bought the fairytale."

"We're going to have to find a replacement for Isabel."

Her eyes filled with tears. "I can't take it anymore. Let's sell the girls and shut down the business."

I ignored her. "Next week is Carnival, and Venice is going to be packed with horny tourists. Don't tell me that you don't have anything planned."

"Sure, there might be a few things . . . but they're all foursomes, I can't imagine that I'd find a girl in time . . . "

"Well, do your best, or you'll be standing in for her."

For a second she was on the verge of getting up and walking out. "I'm forty-one years old, Giorgio," she said calmly. "Don't you think I'm a little old for the whore's life?"

"You're an attractive woman," I shot back with conviction. "And anyway, it's your fucking problem."

She looked down into her bowl and said nothing more until dessert. I even caught a distinct whiff of her despair.

"There's something else that I have to talk to you about, something that concerns you."

"What is it?"

"If I tell you though, you have to promise not to make me do things I don't want to do," she said in an attempt to negotiate. "It's valuable information. Priceless."

"Make you do things? What an unfortunate way of putting it. Anyway, the answer is no."

She gave in and told me anyway. "Brianese is planning to rip you off. Actually, the right term for it would be annihilate you."

I shrugged. "Bullshit, I don't believe that."

"His secretary Ylenia told me."

"I didn't know the two of you were on such close terms."

"She called me up . . . "

"And . . . " I pushed.

"And suggested I work with her to push you out of the business with the girls. She told me that you were through anyway, that you'd become an unpredictable danger."

"But she didn't tell you why?"

"No."

"Still, you accepted."

"You would have done the same thing. She assured me that after the elections you'd have other things to worry about, and that the girls would the last of your worries."

"What did they promise you in exchange?"

"Inside information on certain investments and a position

as the commissioner for cultural affairs in a small town in the province."

"And you act squeamish about working as a hooker in Venice at Carnival?"

"I'm sorry, Giorgio. I know, I should have told you about it before now . . ."

"You're going to keep seeing Ylenia and sending the girls out on jobs for Brianese and his friends. But I want to know everything. No more secrets."

"All right, whatever you say, Giorgio."

I stood up. "Come back at closing time, dressed to kill," I ordered her.

Many hours later, when Gemma opened the door and saw me standing there with Nicoletta, she had a moment of surprise and hesitation. Then she said: "Oh, King of Hearts, you're going to turn me into a bad, bad girl."

Chapter Three
Renegade

When the elections came the Padanos swept to a victory that was beyond anyone's wildest expectations. They were now the absolute masters of nearly every square inch of the Veneto. It was a bitter defeat for Brianese and his party and he was forced to take the blame, like a general who had been beaten on the field of battle. With gnashing of teeth and rending of garments he bravely offered his chest to the firing squad, but it was nothing more than a tableau organized with the local bigwigs and power brokers. They absolved him publicly of all guilt and entrusted him with the task of negotiating with the victors for all the government positions and appointments in the public health department that he could wangle. For that matter, the Counselor was one of the most openly avowed and deeply implicated supporters of the Fearless Leader. There was no way he could climb onto another passing bandwagon. But Brianese had been well aware of that fact for some time now. Every move he made was a stitch in a larger tapestry he was weaving, a strategy designed to allow him to outlive the Fearless Leader and even the party itself, even though he was one of the staunchest defenders of the logic of dynastic succession. The Fearless Leader's daughter was looking like a good prospect.

There was immediate negative fallout on La Nena's business. La Nena was considered the one public venue where the municipal defeat had germinated, and many of our regular customers emigrated elsewhere. The hour of the day when this tendency was clearest was aperitif time, when customers came in to converse and gossip, but the restaurant actually held up well. I immediately decided to take steps. Nicoletta arranged to recruit a certain number of male and female underwear models whose only job was to be seen in the place, behaving like schoolchildren. The evening aperitif hour started livening up again. The long awaited death blow that the Counselor was expected to inflict upon me failed to arrive. I relaxed, in the conviction that he was too busy trying to limit damages. He hadn't been around in a while, nor had any of his colleagues. But really, I was misjudging and underestimating him again.

At the end of a dull spring day, Brianese walked into La Nena with his usual brisk determined step, his usual bright smile stamped firmly on his face. He was jovial and pleasant with everyone and ran through a well-rehearsed routine of wisecracks and personal stories about the Padanos and their mutual adversaries on the center-left.

My stomach did a flip-flop and I only went over to pay my tributes once he'd finished performing his little skit.

"Welcome back, Counselor."

He pretended he'd only just noticed me. "Caro Giorgio, how have you been?" he asked in a loud voice, shaking my hand in delight. "Forgive me if I haven't been around for a while, but here in the Veneto, instead of progressing we're going backwards and no one has time to see their old friends anymore."

Then he locked arms with me and lowered his voice. "Is the back room still 'usable'?"

I smiled with satisfaction. "I never opened it to the public and I've made sure it's nice and clean."

"Perfect. I'm expecting three major enterpreneurs in the food and hospitality industry that I'd like you to meet. I hope you can join us."

"It'll be a pleasure, Counselor."

It became obvious that it would be no pleasure at all the minute I saw them walk into the place. I had no doubt whatsoever that these were Brianese's guests. In all these years, I'd developed a considerable body of experience in terms of the corrupt and the corruptible, profiteers, politicos, businessmen, developers, industrialists, and people who fit into none of those categories. It was clear why the Counselor had chosen not to wait for them at the counter, preferring to go into the back room and loiter there. He didn't want anyone to remember having seen him together with them. I sized them up as they headed straight for the counter. The first one in line had to be the boss, or at least that's what I presumed from the Armani suit. He was about fifty-five years old, roughly five foot six inches in height, with a slight build, salt-and-pepper hair brushed straight back, a square face, a thin nose, and dark eyes set slightly too close together.

The second one was tall and skinny as a reed. His suit was tailor-made but the fabric wasn't exceptionally good. A face out of the Eighties, his hair was a little long over his collar, and he was probably ten years younger than the first guy. He looked like a fugitive from a Spandau Ballet concert.

The guy bringing up the rear was all eyes, looking around and savoring every detail as if it all belonged to him. He was the youngest, the most arrogant, and probably the stupidest of the three. He bore a vague physical resemblance to the first guy, and he wore expensive casual attire that showed off the time he spent in the gym.

I'd seen people like them before, in the exercise yard at San Vittore prison. They always moved in a pack and they considered themselves the masters of the world.

They headed straight for me. "Counselor Brianese," said the boss.

They knew exactly who I was and they'd treated me as if I was a servant. A bad harbinger. I slowly extended my index finger and pointed to the door of the back room. "He's expecting you," I said in the same tone of voice.

I waved over a waitress. Her name was Agata and she was a reliable and likeable employee. Even more important, she was La Nena's corporate memory. She had an unusually accurate photographic memory and was a living archive of every customer that had ever been through the place.

"Have you ever seen them before?"

"The tall one," she answered confidently. "He's been here three or four times recently. By himself."

I pulled a bottle of prosecco out of the fridge and went to find out what a fucked-up trio of Mafiosi accompanied by Brianese was doing in my restaurant.

The Counselor was entertaining them by singing the praises of another parliamentarian whose name I hadn't managed to catch. I poured the wine and waited in silence.

"This is Giorgio Pellegrini, the proprietor." He moved on to introductions once he decided that it was time to talk business.

That's when I found out that the boss was named Giuseppe Palamara, the young guy was Nilo Palamara, Giuseppe's nephew. The beanpole was given short shrift: Bookkeeper Tortorelli.

"These gentlemen have come to meet you because they need to move some fairly substantial sums of money through your restaurant for a while."

A flash of light filled my mind. "Money laundering. They want to turn La Nena into a washing machine."

"Well, my work here is done," the Counselor announced, as he got to his feet. "Now the four of you will certainly have some details to work out that won't require my presence."

None of the others moved a muscle. Everything was proceeding according to script. I waited until Brianese was at the door and then I caught up with him.

"Why are you doing this to me?"

"I'm teaching you what happens when you bite the hand that feeds you."

I was too shocked to think of anything to say. "If those guys get their foot in the door, I'll never get them out of here. They'll take La Nena away from me."

"That'll never happen," he replied. "As I've already told you, you're sick and dangerous, a loose cannon in a system that has very different rules. They'll keep you on a short leash but they'll let you stay where you are."

He could read the rage and hatred in my eyes and a smile played on his lips. He put one hand on my shoulder. "Giorgio, you can't imagine how happy I am right now."

He gripped the handle and opened the door. He hadn't even closed it and he was already greeting someone else. I was just one more problem to him, and I'd been taken care of.

"Come here, Pellegrini," Giuseppe Palamara ordered, accentuating his Calabrian accent.

I turned around and went back to my seat. I filled my glass and drank it off in a single gulp.

"We've asked around about you, and we know all about your time in prison. We know you're an informer, a real piece of shit, and that all you're good for is punching some poor woman in the face who's trying to earn a living," Giuseppe said. "But we also know that you're not so stupid that you can't understand who we are and how far we're willing to go."

I looked at the bottle on the table in front of me. It seemed to have been designed especially to smash into the faces of those bastards. But my hands lay flat on the table, and I heard my voice uttering the words of a slave.

"I know how to stay in my place."

"Good. This is how it's going to work," the boss began explaining. "You can stay in charge of the restaurant, but from now on you're on a salary, and the bookkeeper is going to take care of accounting."

"We'll give you three thousand a month," young Nilo specified.

"Thirty-six thousand a year. It's not bad and you don't have much of a say in the matter."

He rang the tines of a fork against the crystal wine glass to catch my attention. "Understood, Pellegrini? Don't do anything to bring the cops around. No more whores or any of that bullshit. You need to work all day and then go home."

"Understood, Pellegrini?" Giuseppe said again.

"Understood," I replied. "And I assure you that you're really just doing me a favor. This place is just a money pit. I was using all the money I was earning on the girls to pay off the losses here."

Giuseppe Palamara snickered. "Now the bookkeeper will take care of straightening out the books. He's a good accountant and a hard worker. Starting tomorrow morning he's going to sit at that cash register and he's not going to lift his ass out of that chair until the place closes at night."

"That's fine. I'll be able to focus on running this place the way it deserves."

"Good boy," he mocked me. "Now bring us something to eat."

"You still haven't told me how long you plan to use my restaurant."

The Palamaras exchanged an ironic glance. "As long as it takes," Giuseppe answered.

That is to say, forever. After a while they'd persuade me to sell the place, and then they'd probably kill me, as an unasked-for favor to the Counselor. I didn't have any idea what his relationship might be with these Calabrians, but I doubted that he really understood who he was dealing with.

"I'd like to sample the Istrian Malvasia," said Bookkeeper Tortorelli, speaking up for the first time. Up until that moment he'd studied the wine list as if he didn't care about the little lecture the Palamaras were delivering. "You think it would go well with a bowl of *bigoli in salsa*?"

"Personally, it strikes me as a stretch," I replied in a professional tone of voice. "I'd actually recommend a pinot grigio del Collio."

He nodded. "Okay."

I walked out of the back room and stopped Piero, the senior waiter.

"Go take the order from the table in the back room. You're in charge of the restaurant. I have some things to do."

I headed home. I walked briskly, my long steps propelling me down the sidewalk. Martina wasn't there. She was at the gym, attending her Zumba Fitness class. I stripped, putting my clothes away carefully. I dropped into the oxblood red armchair and sat there staring at the spinner bike for a long time—I couldn't say how long. Then my woman got home, said not a word, took off her clothes, climbed onto the bike, and started pedaling. The whisking sound of the roller had a pharmaceutical effect on me, gradually calming all my rage and grief.

The sun was setting when I emerged from the bedroom carrying Martina in my arms. I set her down in the bathtub, turned on the faucet, and planted a kiss on her forehead.

"Thank you, my love. I'll be home as soon as I can."

At the restaurant, there wasn't a trace of the Mafiosi. I warned the staff that starting tomorrow there would be an accountant manning the cash register. Nobody blinked an eye. Nobody would have blinked an eye if I'd told them that La Nena was going to launder dirty money for the Calabrians. These were times when holding onto your job was the only thing that mattered. Everything else was a secondary detail.

I spent the night with Nicoletta. I was implacable, pitiless, and I extracted all the information, down to the tiniest details, that she had gathered over time about the clients who patronized my whores in Brianese's network. But it was a waste of time. I was unable to find anything useful that would improve my understanding of the links between the Counselor and the Palamaras.

"Tell the girls to get ready."

"Are we getting rid of them?" Nicoletta asked hopefully.

"Yes. But I'm going to keep the money," I replied.

She said nothing in reply. She had too much to make up for. And now that we had Mafiosi involved she was willing to do anything I told her, just to get out alive from the nightmare that had begun with Isabel's death. She hadn't figured out yet that I'd never let her go.

The warehouse that served as the Maltese gangsters' headquarters was even filthier than usual. The only thing that glittered in the place was the paint job on the body of my Phaeton.

"Only three this time?" Petrus Zerafa, the boss of the gang, asked me as he massaged the Chinese girl's ass. Lin was looking around in bewilderment. The other two girls were safe in the car. He'd only needed to take a quick look through the window to decide that they were more than acceptable. Lin had struck him as a little skinny and so he'd demanded that she get out so he could inspect the merchandise.

"A Russian guy fell in love and bought one of them," I replied. "It was true love. She wasn't even the prettiest one, but he wouldn't take no for an answer."

"That's not the agreement we had," he protested. "It'll cost you 10 percent."

I expected it. "All right. But you have to throw a handgun with a silencer into the bargain."

He gave me a look. "You don't seem like the type. Are you having problems?"

I did a De Niro imitation. "Do I strike you as someone who has problems?"

He wasn't a stupid guy. "You show up down one whore and

then you ask me to give you a weapon. Maybe something happened and you have to take care of it."

"Do you want to stick your nose into my business or do you want to make a deal?"

He nodded. "I can get you one right away but I don't know how clean it is."

Which meant the gun had been fired and that the police could conceivably link it to a crime. Paradoxically that came in handy, even though it meant I was running the risk of going to jail for something I hadn't even done.

"That's not a problem. All I want is a gun that works, with an extra clip and bullets."

"Lots and lots of ammunition for a guy who doesn't want to kill anyone . . . " he muttered ironically. He gestured to one of his thugs to take care of it and the guy vanished down a tunnel between the mountains of boxes.

Petrus kissed Lin's neck and I understood that the time had come to get rid of the girls. I opened the car door. "Get out."

Dulce and Violeta held hands and sat motionless, pale, and frightened. I stuck my head into the car. "Do whatever they want and it won't go too badly," I advised in a fatherly tone of voice.

Three guys emerged out of nowhere to take delivery of them while Lin remained wrapped in the boss's arms. He'd made his selection.

The guy that had gone to get the pistol came back. He handed me a flat cardboard box that had once held a clock radio. Inside I found a Beretta pistol, thirty years old but well maintained. The ammunition was new, and made by a trusted manufacturer. The silencer was handmade out of a bicycle pump. Zerafa invited me to test it out by shooting into a pile of old tires.

I slipped in the clip and fired three shots in quick succession. The last shot was louder than the others. That meant the silencer filled up fast with smoke. If I had to use it, I'd need to take care to limit my volume of fire.

It felt strange to hold a gun in my hand again after so many years. I'd been certain that guns were alien to me now, but instead my hands had performed the movements correctly and I'd felt the surge of power of my finger on the trigger.

Dulce cried out and I heard the unmistakable sound of a slap. Lin broke free of the Maltese gangster's embrace and threw her arms around my neck, begging me to take her back "home." I pushed her off me with a single hard shove. Petrus burst into laughter and I reminded him that he still owed me money.

He pulled a wad of 500-euro bills out of his jeans pocket and started counting them, after licking the thumb and index finger of his right hand.

I had passed Brescia and I was about to leave Lombardy and enter the Veneto when my cell phone rang.

"Should I be worried?" Tortorelli asked in a bored voice.

"Not at all," I replied with perfect calm. "I'm just shutting down my side business activities, like you asked me to do."

"When will you honor us again with your presence?"

"Tomorrow afternoon, no later than that. In any case, the staff is perfectly capable of running La Nena."

"What would I drink with a plate of frayed dried horse meat with balsamic vinegar and shredded smoked ricotta?"

"A Gewürztraminer would be perfect. It might not be the most orthodox pairing, but you won't be disappointed."

"I took the liberty of telling the cook to skip the bed of arugula. I hate that crap . . . "

"What did the cook do?"

"What I told him. I made him think that it was an order from you."

"You stay away from my kitchen, Tortorelli."

"And you stop playing hide and seek, otherwise there'll be big changes when you get back."

He hung up. Piece of shit. I turned on the radio and turned up the sound to vent my rage. The station was playing a song by Carla Bruni. I caught a line that went: "Someone told me that our lives aren't worth much."

She seemed to be referring to my life. I reached out my hand and caressed the grip of my Beretta. Getting my hands on a weapon meant nothing more than the fact that I was ready to use it. I had no plan, and the ideas in my head were fuzzy at best. The one thing I did know was that unless I reacted I'd lose everything I owned and wind up buried in a shallow grave. Brianese had sold me to the 'Ndrangheta to punish me and keep me under control. He was afraid of me because I'd refused to play by his rules. I could always cut and run for it, abandoning La Nena, Martina, and the life that I'd worked so hard to build for myself, but that wasn't something I was willing to do. I would have run away by now if it was just a fight between yours truly and the Palamaras. In that case I wouldn't have had a whisper of a chance. But Brianese was in the middle of this fight and the only hunch that kept surfacing in the churning whirl of my thoughts, though I still couldn't pin it down, was that there was still a slender margin for negotiation and I might be able to use it to get back what was once mine. I needed to find some form of leverage that would force Brianese to make a deal with me. After all, this was Italy, and by now even the Mafiosi are to some extent obliged to work within the system. In the Veneto, the local and international Mafias had moved in en masse, attracted by a quantity of wealth and an economic system that seemed to have been custom made for money laundering. No one had to be told how it worked: the way they used cutthroat loan sharking practices to take over companies, leaving the owners in place as their puppets while a guy like Tortorelli laundered dirty money and politicians like Brianese forged the right connections to invest that money in government contracts and real estate speculation.

No, it was clear to me that if I wanted to get the Calabrians off my ass I'd have to get the lawyer and member of parliament who'd been the best man at my wedding into the middle of things and use him as leverage. He thought he was above the fray. He'd made his calculations and thought I was done for. And maybe I was, maybe I was deluding myself with my elaborate plans. But Brianese didn't know how much I'd figured out about his relationship with Ylenia and the role that woman played in his web of dealings.

Ylenia. I rolled the name around in my mouth, bouncing it off tongue and teeth. This could be the launching point for my counteroffensive. It could also be a way of clawing back the two million euros that Brianese owed me.

There was a time in my life when I'd been a member of a terrorist group in Italy and later a guerrilla organization in Central America. Before we carried out an operation of any kind we patiently gathered all the information that could be useful and we took the time to plan out the logistics, the escape routes, the emergency plan B. I was going to do the same thing now. The first thing I needed was someone to help me. I could count on Nicoletta but she wasn't enough. The time had come to meet with Mikhail again.

"In two hundred kilometers I'm going to have to stop for gas," I said over the cell phone.

"Do you want to see a picture of my pretty cousin?"

"No."

"Then I'm not sure how interested I am in seeing you."

"Come on, don't be lazy. I'll treat you to a cup of coffee and we can talk a little about Soviet literature."

"Couldn't you have parked in the shadows?" the Russian complained.

I pointed to a closed-circuit camera mounted on a pole. "They've added a new one."

He puffed out his cheeks in annoyance. "All right, what do you need this time? Am I going to have to dig another grave in the countryside?"

"I'm in trouble, Mikhail."

"I'm sorry to hear that but I hope it doesn't involve me in any way."

I pulled the cash from the sale of my three girls out of my pocket and laid the money down next to the stick shift. He peeled off a five hundred euro note and slipped it into his shirt pocket.

"For the trouble of coming out here."

"I need somebody to shadow an 'Ndrangheta bookkeeper like they were glued to him and report all conceivable information back to me," I said, the words tumbling out of my mouth all at once.

"Are you planning to rip off the Calabrian Mafia?"

I shrugged. "That might be an idea, but right now all I want is the information. They're using La Nena to launder dirty money and I want to get them out of there."

"You're crazy," he snickered, reaching out for the door handle.

"I'm not done. I'm also looking for someone with nothing to lose, ready for anything, smart, on the ball, pitiless. You know, a desperate fugitive on the run."

"A renegade."

"That's right."

"And we kill him when the job is done."

"Exactly. And his money would go to you."

"How much are we talking about?"

"Twenty thousand to tail the bookkeeper. Fifty thousand for the renegade."

I monitored his reaction. The money was clearly not enough. "If it all goes according to plan, I ought be able to lay my hands on another 250,000 euros," I lied, thinking about the money that Brianese owed me.

"I don't believe you but theorizing about it's as a good a way as any to kill some time," he said as he lit a cigarette.

"I don't let people smoke in this car." The words slipped out of my mouth.

"Wait: you're thinking about robbing the 'Ndrangheta and killing somebody who's supposed to trust you blindly, but you bust my balls about smoking in your luxury automobile?"

I gestured for him to forget about it and go on. "I can take care of following the guy myself," he said. "And maybe I have a vague idea of who your renegade could be . . . and figuring things on the fly, I don't see how I can do it for less than 200,000 euros."

"You're exorbitant."

"I've never heard the word in my life. Anyway, I may very well be 'exorbitant,' but you're up to your neck in shit."

He had a point. I extended my hand. "You've got a deal."

He shook it, chuckling. "Just remember that I don't trust you even a little bit and that you're never going to be smart enough to rip me off."

He grabbed the wad of cash. "This is my advance. Now tell me who I'm supposed to tail."

The waiters and waitresses were all happy to see me. Tortorelli started off on the wrong foot; he hadn't understood that they had a demanding, exhausting job and deserved to be treated with respect. Things were even worse in the kitchen. I listened and reassured. Then I confronted the bookkeeper.

"Everybody hates you. Nice start."

He carefully watched the ass of a customer as she walked by and I gave him all the time he wanted because that was a piece of interesting information that might help me get a handle on this guy's personality.

"Look, Pellegrini, you're lucky to have me here instead of the Palamaras," he murmured, barely moving his lips. "I'm just a technician and I like to avoid trouble."

"Then I don't see why we should have any problems."

"I take orders from the Calabrians, just like you do, but I outrank you, and hierarchy in this kind of business is the only way of keeping things organized. No one authorized you to do things your way. You're going to have to get it into your fucking head that you have to answer for the things you do and you have ask me permission before you do them. Like the employee that you are."

"Is there anything else?"

"Yes."

"All right. It won't happen again, but I want you to quit meddling in the way the place is run."

"That's a pity, because more than a few changes are needed in the way you're operating here."

He was trying to provoke a reaction and I ignored him. Unintentionally the bookkeeper had just provided me with a useful piece of information: the way the Calabrians had things planned, he was designated to take my place. Tortorelli was ambitious and thought a lot of himself. That much was clear, but nothing else was. He wasn't even Calabrian. Where the fuck did he fit in?

He made me sit there and answer questions, mostly smart ones, for more than an hour. When he asked me what wine went best with Blue Stilton, I intentionally recommended the worst choice imaginable. Maybe that would teach him to stop busting my balls.

A little before the evening aperitif, Nicoletta came in with the owner of a lingerie shop to quench her thirst with an organic carrot juice. I watched Tortorelli, hoping he might show some interest in her. Not only was he indifferent, he made it clear with a wisecrack that he knew she was in charge of my prostitution ring. Brianese had informed them thoroughly.

At the agreed time, the Russian walked into the restaurant. He drank a spritz and impressed the bookkeeper's features clearly in his memory. A short while later, Martina and Gemma came in too, and I was forced to introduce them to Tortorelli. The 'Ndrangheta bookkeeper was courteous and gallant and he was delighted to be invited to sit at their table. The restaurant was full and I had to take care of my customers. I made a mental note to grill the ladies later.

An hour or so later I noticed Gemma get up to go the restroom. She was changing, in fact she was even walking differently. Hurtling down into the abyss of my darkest desires was the best thing that could have happened to her. It was a pity that I'd have to go home to Martina that night.

When I replaced Tortorelli at the cash register at dinnertime I did my best to find any evidence of money laundering. I was curious to figure out how it worked. But I couldn't detect anything out of the ordinary. I spied on him when it was time to shut down the cash register for the night, too, but to no avail.

"Don't forget: tomorrow morning we have an appointment with your accountant to hand over the management of the books," he said before leaving for the night. I watched him through the plate glass window as he walked away into the darkness, the daily receipts stuffed into a cheap briefcase. From that night on, he would be responsible for depositing the money in the night depository. He looked like a perfectly harmless beanpole of a man, strolling through the city streets. Downstairs from my apartment I saw Nicoletta sitting in her car and smoking a cigarette. I walked up to the car window.

"Ylenia was furious when she heard that her boss won't

have access to the whores anymore and she cancelled all our agreements. So long, commissionership."

"Oh, they'd never have kept that promise. Brianese talked to the Calabrians about you, too. You're too tangled up with me to be kept around."

"That bastard!" she hissed, flicking her cigarette butt into the street.

"You can say that loud and clear. And you were his accomplice."

"Don't start that again, Giorgio."

"I'll do exactly the fuck what I want, Nicoletta," I clarified the point for her. "Listen, what do you think about Tortorelli?"

"I don't know. I'd have to get to know him a little better."

"But he's not going to let you get close enough," I cut her off brusquely, handing her a sheet of paper with the address of the residential hotel where Brianese and Ylenia had their lovers' trysts. "Find a way to get me in there. The best thing would be to rent an apartment. Use your brother's real estate agency, fuck every tenant in the building, but don't come back empty-handed."

She clamped another cigarette between her lips. "I put the house up for sale."

"What for?"

She looked at me as if I'd fallen to earth from some other planet. "I watched a girl being murdered on my couch. Have you already forgotten about that?"

"So now you're not comfortable in the place?"

"I go there strictly to sleep at night."

"Move in with Gemma."

She snorted in annoyance. "That girl has some weird ideas in her head. I'd rather not, thanks."

"That wasn't a suggestion, Nicoletta. I just gave you an order."

She started the engine and drove off without saying goodbye. Tortorelli was right about the importance of hierarchies. There were hierarchies for letting off your frustrations, too. Tortorelli took advantage of my subordinate status, and I did the same thing to Nicoletta. And to Martina. And to Gemma. They were essential to my survival. Only the person at the bottom of the pyramid is completely and irremediably fucked. That's why it's so important to find your proper place in the world. Whatever the cost.

Martina asked me if for just one night we could skip the ritual of the creams and ointments.

"Why?"

"I just want to lie here on the bed holding you," she replied in a quavering voice. "I've been so unhappy."

I did as she asked. "There's no other woman. Just business."

She hugged me tight. "The important thing is that you're here with me."

"Let's talk a little," I suggested, knowing that would make her happy.

I deftly steered her toward the subject that interested me. "How's your father?"

"Worse all the time."

"I'm sorry to hear that," I said with a sigh. "I've given a lot of thought to this matter. After all, his illness is having serious repercussions on your mother's and your sisters' lives. I think it's only right to try to do something to make things easier for them."

She propped herself up on her elbow to look at me. "What do you mean?"

"I talked to a client of mine who's a doctor. I asked him to find out the name of the best medical center in Europe for this condition and he told me about a clinic in Lahnstein, Germany. Apparently they're miracle workers."

"That would be wonderful."

"I'll pay for everything and you and your mother could take your father to Germany. There are residential hotels that rent apartments for the patients' families."

Martina was deeply moved, and I mentally said a word of thanks to the Internet. I'd had no idea how to get Martina out of harm's way, but then it occurred to me that maybe I could take advantage of her father's sickness. I goggled the word "Alzheimer's" and looked around for a clinic somewhere in the deepest countryside. I found it in a little town in Rhineland-Palatinate.

"But we'd have to be apart for such a long time. At least a month, if not longer," she said in a worried voice. "You have so much work to do with La Nena . . . "

I put a finger against her lips. "Hush. You're just worried that I might sleep with other women. We already had that conversation a while ago, or am I mistaken?" I snapped out in a harsh voice.

"No, you're not mistaken."

"And what did you promise me?"

"That I would try to be strong."

I gave her a kiss. "You know that I love only you, baby doll of mine."

I moved away from her in the bed and tried to get comfortable and fall asleep. That wasn't what Martina was expecting, and it would upset her, but only a little. The next morning she'd try to find out if something she'd said or done had made me mad. I'd be intentionally evasive and then I'd pretend to take umbrage. An excellent way to start the day before dealing with that asshole the bookkeeper.

As we left my accountant's office, Tortorelli informed me that I would be changing all my suppliers. He pulled a list of the new suppliers out of his inside jacket pocket. I'd never heard of any of them.

"But are they good suppliers?" I asked naïvely.

"From our point of view they're the very best suppliers, Pellegrini."

"If the quality of the restaurant declines, we all stand to lose."

"No, actually only you do," he replied in a flat voice. "Because you'll look like an asshole who doesn't know how to run his own place. As far as we're concerned, if we lose customers and have to reduce expenses and staff, that's better."

He forced me to cross the street and drink an espresso in a café run by the Chinese. It was practically empty except for a couple behind the counter, an Asian playing a slot machine for losers, and a table full of little old men playing cards.

He pointed to the serial number on the receipt. "These guys don't even pretend to have turnover or customers," he explained. "They launder a million euros with the clear understanding that they're going to lose thirty percent. Six months later they let the Italians take over management again and the bar starts operating normally again. We don't work that way, and at the very most we take a loss of fifteen percent. But we more than make that back by investing the money we've laundered in the public works sector."

"I'm not sure I understand exactly what you mean."

"Talking to you is just a waste of time, Pellegrini. The important thing is that you understand that we aren't the Chinese mob and that laundering money is both an art and a science."

We went back to La Nena and in just a few hours I realized for the first time that I'd become a marionette. A sense of shame began to wash over me and I felt an intolerable wave of embarrassment. My one slender reed of hope lay in the natural acceleration of events that crime creates in the routine progress of life. For eleven years nothing noteworthy had happened. Then a series of events, beginning with Brianese stealing two million euros from me, had made negative changes in my life that trended toward its ultimate destruction. It was only a matter of time. But now my "criminal" reaction would trigger a new and unpredictable acceleration of events. That was my science, and killing was my art. I sighed and secretly hoped that I'd soon have an opportunity to show Tortorelli the precision and beauty of what I knew how to do.

Something important happened the following day, when I got a phone call from an officer at my bank who specialized in investments. He wanted to compliment me on the steady growth of revenue, which was growing by about a thousand euros a day. He asked if we could meet to examine a financial plan.

That's how I discovered that the bookkeeper was adding money to the day's take before taking it to the night depository. More or less thirty thousand euros a month. More money was coming in through the network of suppliers. It added up to about a million or 1.5 million euros a year. He must have other resources, otherwise it made no sense to take over a restaurant and put a man there full time.

But the interesting fact was that Tortorelli had a vault somewhere he was getting cash out of. And the first thing that occurred to me is that vaults are made to be filled up and then emptied.

Mikhail got in touch four days later, in the afternoon. Gulping uncomfortably, afraid to face Tortorelli's sardonic smirk, I was forced to ask the bookkeeper for permission to leave the restaurant.

"What could you possibly have to do that's so important?" the bastard took pleasure in asking.

"Family problems."

"Ah, if the family's involved go right ahread, but be back in time for dinner. I don't feel like getting stuck here."

As I was pulling onto the highway it started to rain and,

shortly thereafter, to hail. I sped up in search of a bridge to take shelter under. A few miles at 100 mph and I found one, but it was too late to save the body from dents. I got back in the car and drove on, indifferent to the pelting ice pellets. My former lawyer or the Palamaras would pay for the bodywork.

The service plaza was more crowded than usual. As soon as I parked the Russian pulled open the passenger side door and sat down beside me.

"A luxury vehicle is only beautiful if it's immaculate," he launched into a philosophical riff. "Otherwise it's a blight on the landscape. It triggers a Russian's inborn melancholy."

I rubbed my eyes. "You have something more interesting to tell me, don't you, Mikhail?"

He smiled. "Tortorelli comes from Pero, on the outskirts of Milan," he began. "He has no criminal record, he owned a food services company that went bankrupt three years ago. He's divorced, and he has two high-school-aged boys. His ex-wife is in a new relationship with a local small businessman."

"You got this information from the deputy commissioner of police who offers protection to the two Neapolitan ex-hookers you work for."

"I called in a favor," he admitted.

"It doesn't strike me as particularly valuable."

"Well, it's useful to put our man into context," he hedged in self-justification. "He lives in a suite in a hotel operated by a company with ties to the Palamaras."

"Which one?"

"The Negresco Palace."

I knew the place. It opened for business recently, all glass and cement. A nondescript four-star hotel on the outskirts of town, not far from the highway. A number of them had been springing up recently, after the expansion of the trade fair's exhibition space. I wondered if the Calabrians' vault was there.

"The bookkeeper spends all his time in your restaurant,"

the Russian went on. "I followed him at night and in the morning. It wasn't hard. He's definitely a creature of habit. When he leaves La Nena he walks to Piazza Vittoria di Lepanto and catches a cab from there to the Negresco Palace. In the morning, he takes a cab back to the piazza, does a few errands, and then goes to work."

"Doesn't he ever have sex?"

"He calls out and has whores sent up to his hotel room."

"That's all? You didn't find anything else?" I asked in disappointment.

"There's only one odd detail," said the Russian, finally coming to the point. "Every Monday the cab that picks him up in the piazza is from a limo service."

"A limo service," I echoed him. "Not a medallion cab, a private service."

Mikhail's lips twisted into a sardonic smile that reminded me, for just a second, of a French actor. "It's always the same driver, and he always has the same car, a Lexus sedan with a gray metallic finish. But here's the thing: the car drives all the way here from Milan, just to take Tortorelli to his hotel."

"How do you know?"

"I followed him. He dropped off the bookkeeper and went right back to the limo company office."

"You know what I think? I think that driver is so generous that he just makes the rounds of the various Tortorellis and gives each of them a big fat envelope full of cash."

"You think?"

I told him about the unprecedented steady growth in turnover at La Nena. "You remember when you asked if I'd decided to rip off the 'Ndrangheta? Well, the way things are going, it's starting to look like a distinct possibility."

"Then you're going to need a renegade with big square balls, as you Italians like to say." The sly smile had reappeared on his face.

"I'll bet you've found me one."

He stuck his hand out the window and waved it as if he was signaling to someone. A few seconds later the rear door opened and a man got into the car. I looked up into the rearview mirror.

"Hey, asshole," I shouted. "Get out of my car."

The Russian put a hand on my arm. "It's him."

I jerked around to get a better look at him. "But he's black."

"My name is Hissène and I'm African. I come from Chad," he corrected me in excellent Italian, spoken with a strong French accent.

"It's a pleasure to meet you, but I still don't understand what the fuck you're doing in my car."

The Chadian opened the door and spoke to Mikhail. "I think the two of you may need to talk things over. Why don't I wait outside?"

"Why were you so rude to him?" the Russian scolded me.

"Because this is the Veneto and even the traffic cops are on the hunt for illegal immigrants," I answered indignantly. "He's just the right color to attract plenty of the kind of attention we definitely don't want."

"You're not thinking about it the right way."

"Why not?"

"Because there's no way to trace him back to you, and whatever it is you're planning to do, you're going to have to look innocent *afterward*," he replied, speaking slowly and emphatically. "Let's say we actually decide to steal from the Calabrians . . . What better way to deflect suspicion than having a black guy pull the job?"

"What do you know about him?"

"He was a drug courier for the Nigerian mafia, but he decided to keep the condoms filled with heroin and sell them."

"So he's a dead man walking."

"Exactly. They'll just blame other Africans for his death."

Put in those terms, the whole thing was worth taking into consideration, even though I still had enough objections that I doubted it would work out. "We can only use him when it's time to get tough. We can't think of using him for stakeouts or tailing people."

"I'll take care of that business."

"How did you find him?"

"I'm a foreigner myself and I was an illegal immigrant before being hired by the Neapolitans . . . let's say that I know that world."

I stepped out of the car and waved to him to get in. "I owe you an apology," I started cobbling together an excuse, "but you caught me off guard. I didn't expect you to be black." He looked at me without expression.

"Can I ask you a few questions?"

"That depends."

"Do you know how to shoot?"

"In 2006 I fought for the UFDC to overthrow President Idriss Déby Itno. I'm one of the very few survivors of the march on Ndjamena."

"I don't know what you're talking about. But I think you're telling me yes."

"Kalashnikov rifles, Makarov pistols, RPGs . . . " he reeled off in a weary voice. "The usual checklist of any African war."

I pointed to the Russian. "Did he tell you how much you'd be paid?"

"Fifty thousand and a passport."

The passport was just a new lie that Mikhail had added to the pile. I observed him closely. Hissène was young and strong. And he had a handsome, slightly effeminate face with particularly long eyelashes.

"How old are you?"

"Twenty-nine."

"Do you have a place to stay?"

"No place that's secure," he replied. "You're going to have to take care of that."

Actually, I did have a place to hide him, one where I could always keep an eye on him. Use him and then, after taking the appropriate precautions, steer him toward his ultimate fate.

I stuck out my hand. "Okay. You're enlisted."

He took my hand reluctantly. He didn't trust me. The fact that he was still alive after stealing from the Nigerians meant he wasn't that big of a fool. I waved to him to get out of the car. "Do you mind? I have to talk a few things over with my partner."

I worked it out with Mikhail that I would take delivery of the Chadian on the following night. I needed a little time to take care of his lair.

"In the meantime I need you to get all the information you can about the Lexus," I told him. "If it actually is carrying a wad of cash from Lombardy then there's a good chance we'll have a nice chunk of cash on our hands."

"Next Monday I'll see if I can follow it down from Milan."

"Don't ask your cop anything else about him," I warned him. "He could get curious and greedy."

"Don't worry. I don't need him anymore."

It was time for me to get back to work, to keep from arousing Tortorelli's suspicions. I was satisfied and hopeful. At last the outlines of a plan were beginning to take shape. I started out with an intuition about Ylenia Mazzonetto, Brianese's secretary. Now I knew a lot more and I had a ragtag little army at my command, maybe sufficient for what I had in mind. I had to figure out how to get all the characters to read from the same script. And get out of this alive. It wouldn't be easy but it was too late to turn back now: the criminal acceleration of events had reached cruising velocity.

As I got closer to La Nena I noticed that something was

missing. Or rather, that someone was missing. Ding Dong, the bouncer I paid to keep street vendors out of the restaurant, wasn't manning his usual post. His nickname was a humorous reference to his mental state—tenuous at best. The section of portico that the front door looked out upon and the large plate glass window of the restaurant were his second home. His first home was his mother's place, but he and she didn't get along and he couldn't wait to take up his post by the front door every day and ward off unwanted visitors.

I should have guessed that Tortorelli would have something to do with it. "I sent him away."

"Why would you do that?" I asked in horror. "Now there's going to be an endless procession of flower vendors and panhandlers of all kinds, busting the customers' balls."

"People are used to it. And it was a question of courtesy."

"Courtesy?"

"Courtesy toward the person who manages them," he explained as if he was talking to a mental defective.

Disheartened, I went to take shelter in the kitchen to talk with the cook.

Around lunchtime the shithead told me that he'd be eating lunch in another restaurant. A buffet was being held to celebrate the successful outcome of Brianese's political negotiations concerning positions in the health department. He'd managed to obtain 45 percent of the offices, even though the Padanos were furious at discovering that numerous bank accounts were in the red while the ledgers recorded them as being in the black.

"And he invited you to come?"

"No, but I figured I'd drop by just to show my face. And to learn a little something. At that other restaurant they know how to choose the right wine for a Blue Stilton."

I couldn't help but smile. He raised his index finger. "One time," he said in a solemn voice. "You can make a fool of me just once."

"You are definitely quite the hard-ass," I mocked him.

"Keep it humble, Pellegrini. The longest dick is stuck firmly up your ass right now."

"You know, I really don't understand the things you say."

"I know that. You're so stupid it almost makes me pity you." Just then a cruel desire flashed through my mind with the power and speed of an uppercut. I squinted to enjoy the thought more thoroughly and Tortorelli misunderstood it as a gesture of surrender.

"I'll never understand why the Honorable Brianese ever decided to put all this trust in you," he added in a disgusted tone. Then he went back to his place behind the cash register. I hurried down to the cellar to look for a special bottle.

I put it down in front of Tortorelli. "A peace offering."

He looked at me scornfully. "Fine. Thanks very much. Now I have to get back to work."

I ran my finger over the surface of the bottle. "Notice how thick the glass is. It has to contain pressure of up to ten atmospheres. Look at the beautiful line, the way it runs from the neck down to the base."

"It's just an ordinary bottle, so what?"

"It's a *prestige cuvée* champagne bottle," I corrected him. "The queen of bottles."

"I'll drink it to your health," he said sarcastically.

"See, now you're the one who doesn't understand," I said in a mysterious tone before going back to taking care of reservations.

I was sorry I'd treated the bookkeeper that way. I was clearly worn out from the tension and last night I hadn't managed to get back my equilibrium. I blamed Nicoletta. When I told her that she was going to have to go back home and play nursemaid to a Chadian refugee and explained that she was going to get even deeper into a situation where yet another person was going to get badly hurt, she kind of spun out of control. I was forced to become very persuasive. It demanded a lot of work and it took most of the night. I only had time enough to take a shower, and I was forced to forego the extraordinary force of Martina's devotion. That was my last shot at it before shutting down operations for a good long while. In fact, at that very moment, she was already traveling toward the German clinic where she was going to help her mother care for her sick father.

"Think about me," she said, as she told me goodbye at the door.

I'd have to make do with Gemma, but she was still green. We didn't have the kind of complicity that only time can nurture between two people.

At the end of a dull day I managed to get away from the restaurant and make it to my appointment with Mikhail, to take the Chadian to his new and final home.

Hissène traveled light. A tiny shoulder bag with a couple of T-shirts and some underwear. He climbed into the car without a word. I stayed outside to talk briefly with the Russian.

"I'm starting to hear complaints from the Neapolitans," he said in a worried voice. "I'm away too much."

"On Monday, you follow the Lexus and then we'll move."

"So you have a plan?"

"Sure," I lied, for no reason.

"This is Nicoletta. She's your fairy godmother, she'll take care of you."

The African was surprised to find himself looking at an elegant white woman and a house that was palatial by his standards.

My former partner held out a hand and he shook it awkwardly. "I'm Hissène."

She looked at me. "Did you explain the rules to him?"

The Chadian beat me to it. "I can't go out and I can't let

myself be seen through the windows, don't use the home phone . . . I know the rules better than both of you, I live in hiding."

"You're going to have to be patient. Before we act we still have a couple of things to check out."

"I'm in no hurry," he said, pointing to the sofa where I'd strangled Isabel. "I'll just get comfortable and watch some satellite TV."

He pointed to the stairs. "Where's my bedroom?"

"Come on, I'll show you," said Nicoletta.

I poured myself a drink. Just a drop of amaro. There were a lot of discotheques in that area and plenty of cops with breathalyzers. She came back downstairs after a few minutes.

"I'm going to be afraid to be alone with him."

"We already talked about that," I said brusquely. "Any news about the residential hotel?"

She pulled a bunch of keys and a remote control out of her purse. "There's an apartment, directly underneath the one where Ylenia and Brianese fuck, and it's free from Friday afternoons until Monday mornings. The structural engineer who uses it returns home for the weekends and all major holidays."

"I expected something better."

A note of exasperation crept into her voice. "You always think that all you have to do is dominate other people's lives and snap your fingers to get whatever you want. That's not how it works."

"You've been whining since last night."

"Because I can't do this anymore."

"Do what? Betray your partners?" I mocked her.

She jabbed her index finger into my chest. "I'm not Martina and I'm definitely not that nutjob Gemma."

"Calm down. You have a guest."

"You have to give me a way out, Giorgio, or I'm not going to give a damn what I do next."

"Seriously?"

"Don't doubt me."

I knew her too well to think that she was just talking. I sat down and pointed to the bottle of amaro and the empty glass.

"Pour me a drink."

Nicoletta did as she was told. She lit a cigarette and blew the smoke toward the ceiling. In my previous life I'd met another woman who slid through my fingers. She decided she wouldn't take any more, she rebelled against me, and I lost her forever. Women like that are strange. Once they make up their minds, they don't look back. They're willing to pay any price, no matter how extreme. The woman in front of me was ready to flush everything and everyone down the toilet. I had to accept it and just forget about toying with her life. What a pity. Now the only thing left to do was to try to negotiate terms that wouldn't make me look like a fool. Everthing has a price, and I'd make sure she paid the highest possible price.

"Anything I tell you to do until this business is out of the way," I ventured, without taking a breath. I paused for a beat. Then I spread my hands slowly. "Then each of us goes our own way. You can leave the city and I never want to see you again."

"You've got a deal."

I spread my legs and settled back, getting comfortable. "When people make a deal, there should be a celebration."

"Right," she said, sinking to her knees. "Maybe after I'm done with you I'll do the black guy too, just for fun," she added in a tone of voice I didn't particularly like.

"He might not throw himself at your feet, white goddess," I shot back viciously. "You're at least ten years older than him."

Gemma had an old record player and a collection of vinyl LPs that her husband hadn't been able to take south with him when he left. Every so often I rummaged through the albums and picked out ones that were crucial to the history of my generation. Records I listened to when I was a young dickhead and wanted to start a revolution. I listened to Jefferson Airplane's *Volunteers*. I'd fallen head over heels for the lead singer, Grace Slick. She was an outrageous babe and she had a warm contralto voice that always gave me a hard-on. Now the new diamond-tip needle that I'd asked my fuck buddy Gemma to buy finally did justice to a well-preserved vinyl copy of *Manhole*, her first solo album. I didn't miss those years in the slightest. Still, there was one good thing to say about that period. Compared to the present, young people had a lot of fun showing the world how ridiculous it was. There was an astounding wave of creativity in every field, from music and film to art and crime. Extraordinary gangs of armed robbers had cleaned out bank vaults with great rock music echoing in their ears and a joint on their lips. Someone in my group of acquaintances had even begun theorizing the concept of creative criminality and contrasting it with the cruel, dull, repetitive crimes committed by the capitalist establishment. What complete horseshit.

I lifted a foot and jammed it between Gemma's thighs. She was dangling exhausted from the ceiling. We'd played astronaut, and I've rarely seen a woman have such an intense orgasm that she went into a brief state of complete delirium. I slowly ran my foot down the length of her leg, and then gave her foot a sharp push so she spun around dizzily.

In those days, organized crime was more effervescent and less oppressive. Evidently even the major crime gangs were affected by the changes sweeping through the world. Then, when the collective dream came to an end and there was a mass of losers in prison doing life without parole, the various international Mafias moved in and globalization decimated any free market competition, so that the sphere of illegal pursuits turned gray and humdrum like everything else.

People like the Palamaras were exactly the same thirty

years ago. They were dinosaurs who'd always lived in a culture devoid of any imagination. We on the other hand chanted "all power to the imagination!" I think Marcuse was the one who came up with that chestnut. I stood up and turned over the LP.

"Hey, King of Hearts," Gemma murmured. "Will you fuck me again?"

I took a look down there. Not a chance. "The kitchen's closed."

"Take another tablet."

I'd taken a good deal more than the maximum dose of the blend of Cialis and Peruvian *maca*. "One more milligram could kill me," I mumbled.

Where was I? I asked myself. I didn't want to lose the thread of my thoughts about imagination because that was exactly what I needed to screw the Calabrians. I knew their way of thinking. I remembered a number of episodes from my time in jail when whoever happened to be capo at the time veered out of control because someone or something had upset the sacrosanct Mafia routine.

Manhole was a convulsively sensual piece of music. I felt a slow, sinuous discharge of shivers up and down my back. Why the fuck had I deprived myself of that absolute beauty until now? I lifted my leg again and sent my girlfriend's body spinning around.

Another flash. *Knock Me Out*. Another great song by Grace Slick and Linda Perry.

Confusion new
Do you, and nothing's right . . .

Confusion. Chaos. Breakdown. Hurly-burly. A Russian, an African, an Italian. It sounded like the beginning of a joke, but it might turn out to be the basis for a creative crime that I could test out on the Calabrians. *Confusion*. I'd have to stun them with creativity. Blind them with imagination.

The supposed invincibility of the Mafia was a truth tarnished by numerous exceptions. Proof of that fact was given by the fairly high number of punitive murders.

Do you feel like giving it a try? I asked myself.

Grace Slick ran me through with a high note and I reached out my hand to grab Gemma's ass, certain that independent operators like me still had a right to dream of the future.

The next morning I woke up filled with healthy energy, waiting for the end of a dull day when the Russian would bring me the information that I needed.

He didn't disappoint me. He'd worked like a professional. He'd followed the Lexus without being noticed. He'd jotted down a bewildering variety of notes, on places, schedules, mileage, location of security cameras, physical descriptions, license plate numbers, and car models.

"I'm pretty sure we can do this," I said when he was done.

"Of course we can," the Russian retorted. "The problems are going to start once we hurt them. They're going to want to take revenge, but that's going to be your problem. I'm going to be long gone. Everybody needs to be afraid of their own personal Mafia."

"Are you afraid of yours?"

"So afraid that I'll never go back to Russia."

"Then where are you planning to go?"

He looked at me as if I was a drooling idiot. "Venezuela, where else? The birthplace of my lovely prostitutes."

We celebrated with Coca-Cola and puff pastries at the bar in the service plaza. At that time of night, they'd stopped selling alcohol to keep young kids from driving into a bridge abutment at 125 mph in daddy's BMW.

CHAPTER FOUR
Ylenia

That residential hotel was so discreet that even the elevator ran silently. When the sliding doors opened, with an almost imperceptible whoosh, Ylenia would never expect me to be waiting for her. I took a step forward and placed the muzzle of the silencer just beneath her right eye.

I uttered the magic words: "If you scream I'll kill you."

I pushed the button for the floor below. The woman was paralyzed with terror and I took advantage of the fact to shove her down the hallway and into the structural engineer's apartment: I'd left the front door ajar so I wouldn't be forced to fool around with keys.

Brianese's secretary turned around to face me, and that's when I punched her in the stomach with a left hook. I needed to make sure I knocked the breath out of her so she couldn't scream. She fell to the floor in a sitting position. I jammed a rubber toy ball for dogs into her mouth. Then I grabbed her by the hair and dragged her into the exercise room. I ripped her clothes off and tied her on all fours to the weight bench.

During my time in Central America I'd learned that when soldiers capture a guerrilla fighter and want to get information out of him, they torture him immediately, to avoid letting any interval of delay give him time to accept his situation as a prisoner and construct psychological defenses. French, American, and Israeli military advisers had crisscrossed the planet teaching this one important truth.

Ylenia was neither a political militant nor a woman of the

underworld. She was a secretary who had come of age in the shadow of a powerful man like Brianese. She'd learned to be cunning and arrogant, but she knew absolutely nothing about violence.

I sat down in front of her, picked up a solid chrome barbell, and I started applying Vaseline to the tip. She started writhing as if she were having convulsions, but I'd tied her up securely. Her eyes were a mess of mascara and tears. Snot was running out of her nose. She pissed herself, and it dribbled onto the floor.

"If I stick this into you," I started explaining, "by the time I'm done you'll be so torn up inside that the emergency room doctors would be hard pressed to keep you alive. I'd have no choice but to finish you off, chop you up, and feed you to the hogs. Just think of the headlines: 'Secretary of Member of Parliament Sante Brianese Vanishes into Thin Air' . . . You'd just be one of those unsolved missing person cases they talk about on television." I imitated the well-known moderator of a program specializing in unsolved mysteries and cold cases. "Still no new leads in the disappearance of Ylenia Mazzonetto . . . "

I put my mouth close to her ear. I wanted her to feel the heat of my breath. "But if you tell me about Brianese's dirty business dealings I'll let you go. No one, not even him, will ever know that you betrayed him. I don't want to ruin him, I just want to take back La Nena. My sole desire is for you and the Counselor to become my best customers again, with friendship and harmony reigning uncontrasted between us."

I picked up the weights bar again and walked around behind her. I barely touched her and she shuddered. "Now I want you to nod your head. Yes or no. It's entirely up to you, Ylenia."

She didn't have a moment's hesitation. She was ready, right then and there, to betray anyone to save herself. I set up the tripod and video camera that I'd just purchased in a superstore.

I placed them so that her face filled the frame. I pulled the ball out of her mouth.

"Talk," I ordered her.

She was in shock and the words that came out of her mouth barely made sense. I slapped her. "Start with the last dirty deal," I recommended in a fatherly tone of voice.

At first her voice quavered and shook. Then she gradually became just a bit more confident. She told me that Brianese had plunged heart and soul into the nuclear power business. His job was to lay the political and legislative groundwork. He was supposed to tour the Veneto with hired scientists to lay out the benefits of nuclear power as an energy source and to identify the ideal sites.

"I don't see who benefits."

"The operation is being financed by lobbyists on behalf of a corporation that sells obsolete nuclear power plants that other governments have phased out. The objective is to sell them as if they were the latest design, and then drag out construction delays indefinitely to postpone safety inspections and suck as much money as possible out of the system."

I pretended not to believe her so she'd be forced to give me more details. "Now you're just pulling my leg," I snapped out in a harsh tone as I grabbed the barbell.

"No! I swear every word is true," and she started reeling off names and details.

Brianese called while his secretary was giving me embarrassing details about internal party relations. I paused the video camera, took her cell phone out of her purse, and held it up to her ear. I used the other hand to point the silenced handgun at her temple.

"Tell him that something unavoidable came up and you're running late. Pull some bullshit and you'll die, and I'll send this lovely piece of video to mommy and daddy, as well as to the press."

"All right."

I pushed the button that let her talk to her lover. "Sorry Sante, I had a problem with my car . . . No no, wait for me, I'll be there soon, ciao . . . ciao."

She hadn't been all that convincing, but there'd been no way of dodging that phone call. I had to move quickly. I turned off her cell phone and put it back in its place.

"Just think how cruel life can be, Ylenia," I mocked her. "Your beloved is right upstairs, worrying about why you're late, and here you are, just a few feet away, digging him a shallow grave."

She burst into desperate sobs. I'd committed an error. Now it would be harder to extort information from her, but I already had enough to blackmail the secretary and start negotiations with the Counselor.

I waved the toy ball for dogs in front of her eyes. "Stop it, or I'll plug your mouth and hurt you badly, so very badly."

"Let me go. I've told you everything."

"Nonsense. But it's enough for now. I only have a couple more personal questions."

I started the video camera back up. "How long have you been sleeping with Brianese?"

"Seven years."

"I'm sure he's the love of your life," I commented. "Does his wife know about it?"

"I think she does, but she doesn't care. They haven't had sex in years."

"And just how is the Counselor in bed?"

"Don't ask me that, I beg you."

"But that's the most interesting part. If you like, I can help you remember," I said, reaching up to unzip my trousers.

That was enough. She answered every question. She didn't skip the slightest detail. When I turned off the video camera, Brianese had no secrets from me. All that was left were the questions that concerned me directly.

"Why did he decide to ruin me and take away La Nena?"

The answer really caught me by surprise. "He can't pay you the two million euros he owes you."

"It's not because I broke into his house and got blood all over his raincoat?"

She shook her head. "Sante's drowning in debt."

"With all the money he can lay his hands on?"

"He's saving his party singlehandedly, laying the foundations for the future, when they'll be able to take back the Veneto."

"Just where do the Palamaras come from?"

"They're doing construction all across Lombardy, but there's a group of magistrates that are conducting a money laundering investigation. So they decided to move things into the Veneto."

"How did they first make contact?"

"One of their construction companies won a contract for a new highway. There was bid-rigging involved . . . "

Ylenia was done. I could stick a fork in her now. It was time to hand her back to her master, lover, mentor, father . . . "So what is a girl from a nice family like yours doing with a corrupt politico like Brianese?"

"Sante's not corrupt," she retorted indignantly. "It's not his fault that being in politics these days forces him to wallow in the mud. He wants what's best for this country, but he has to deal with reality."

I'd been right. She was head over heels in love and she had swallowed whole every last tissue of horseshit that the Counselor had foisted off on her. He'd turned her into a docile and useful tool. I was an expert on the subject, so I was pretty sure I wasn't wrong. That's why I took care to avoid mentioning the fact that her beloved Sante had always made ample and regular use of my prostitution ring. He had doubtless told her that he never did anything but accompany others, keeping his dick safe and dry in his trousers, because he loved and desired her and only her. Those were the same words I would have used to hornswoggle her. If I told her the whole truth, it would make the dam burst. Ylenia would be no more use to me. In fact, she'd be a menace.

I patted her on the cheek. "In spite of everything he's done, I'm persuaded that the Counselor is a decent, respectable man myself. That's just one more reason why he should never find out about this little chat we've had. Right?"

I took the key to the apartment out of her purse and made a mould of it in soft plasticine. It could turn out to be useful. I went back into the exercise room and untied her, pushed her into the bathroom, and stuck her under a cold shower. Before leaving the apartment I held the little video camera under her nose. She was a complete mess. Her face was a rigid mask. Both her blouse and skirt were slightly torn and tattered. "I have no idea of what you're going to tell him, but you'd better be convincing."

I forced her to ride down to the garage with me in the elevator. I gave her a kiss on the cheek and got into the little runabout that Agata, one of the waitresses, had loaned me.

I got back to the restaurant a few minutes after nine. The first round of tables was already being served dessert.

Tortorelli crooked a finger for me to come over to the cash register.

"I'm getting pretty steamed at you," he hissed.

"You talk like my grandfather."

"Now you've gone too far. Next week I'm going to tell Giuseppe Palamara about the crap you've pulled. You'll see: he'll cure you of the desire to be a smartass."

I looked around the dining room. A Pakistani street vendor was making the circuit of the tables, laying flowers on the linen napkins and interrupting the diners' conversations.

"I'm starting to think about selling the place," I grumbled. "Do you think that Signor Palamara might be interested?"

The bookkeeper changed his attitude and became much more conciliatory. "I have no doubt," he replied. "Have you already thought about what to do next?"

"Leave town and get into another line of business. My wife has already moved to Germany to take care of her father . . . "

The shithead nodded understandingly. He was picturing himself running La Nena.

"I guess I could open a pizzeria around Duisburg. I've heard that Signor Palamara knows people in that part of the country."

The sarcasm was lost on him. "If you like I could talk to him about it."

"Really? You'd be doing me a favor."

I made the rounds of the tables, unobtrusively observing his reaction. He appeared to be satisfied and relieved. He expected to receive a pat on the back from his employers and to be given a decent position at last. He'd give up his hotel room and move into an apartment and see if he could find a girlfriend among the clientele. At last, a ray of sunshine in his life. Too bad I'd made other plans for him.

It was a long, tiring evening. My customers could feel spring coming and they felt like staying up late. Before going over to Gemma's house I went home and downloaded the video into my computer. I'd take care of editing it properly later. I'd cut out the questions. Ylenia had been perfect. As long as she didn't cave in and tell Brianese everything. I was pretty sure she wouldn't.

"King of Hearts! At last you're here," my hostess greeted me.

"I'm deeply horny tonight," I warned her. "I had an opportunity to have some fun with a pretty young thing but I was forced to refrain out of prudence."

"Not a consideration when it comes to me, I assure you."

"Absolutely not."

"Do you think I might be a worthy substitute for the pretty young thing?"

"I think it's fair to give you a chance to try."

On Sunday afternoon, immediately after lunch, I went back to the residential hotel to eliminate all evidence of my stay in the structural engineer's apartment. I came equipped with everything needed for an in-depth cleaning job. As soon as I drove into the underground garage I noticed Ylenia's Mini Cooper convertible. Out of caution, I made sure that the Counselor's car wasn't parked somewhere out of sight, but I was pretty sure that on Sunday afternoon he was spending time with his wife, family, and friends. This was the day of the week dedicated to family, and Brianese would never have made an exception.

Curiosity led me to push the doorbell of their love nest. She opened the door with a radiant smile, certain it was her beloved Sante. She turned white as a sheet and her first impulse was to slam the door in my face, but the tip of my shoe was too fast for her. I shoved her inside. She was wearing an ivory-colored slip. A little old-fashioned, the way the Counselor liked it.

"What are you doing here?" I asked. "On a Sunday you ought to be with mommy and daddy or with your girlfriends. Attending Mass, bringing trays of pastries, tagliatelle and roast chicken . . . "

"I preferred to stay here."

"Problems with your lover?" I asked, looking around the place. The apartment was decorated with good taste, in an expensive rustic style. This was no sex dive: it really was a love nest.

"He didn't believe me," she replied in a tone of lament. "He's convinced I had hot sex with a young lover."

"Hot sex." I snickered as I imagined the scene. "The Counselor's jealous."

She gave me a look filled with hatred. I handed her the

plastic bag filled with cleansers and sponges of all kinds. "Come on down with me and help clean up your pee stains from yesterday. While we work I can fill you in on how men operate."

In her slip and pink elbow-length rubber gloves, Ylenia looked like a porn star in a movie about sexy housewives. While she was down on her knees cleaning the floor a lock of hair fell over her eyes and she tossed her head with a fairly sexy movement. As promised, I was generous with information. I told her plenty of secrets about us men and gave her a heap of advice, most of it useless, about how to win back her Counselor. It was fun and relaxing. She listened attentively, nodding now and then, and other times peering over at me in bafflement. When I accompanied her back upstairs, I felt sure that I'd created a feeling of companionship with the pretty young secretary.

"I was lucky I met Sante," she said as she walked into the apartment. "By now I could have been married to someone like you. Someone ignorant and violent."

Lightning flashes of mute fury exploded in my eyes, blinding me for a second or two. I concentrated on the shape of a table lamp to keep from doing something foolish. "Just wait a few years. You won't be his lover anymore. You'll be his caregiver," I hissed, certain that that one would put her down for the count.

"Ah, the ripening maturity of my gerontophilia."

"What the fuck did you just say?"

"Nothing important, but don't start acting all buddy-buddy. You kidnapped me and threatened to kill me in order to extort information out of me and I was afraid to resist."

"Don't get a swelled head. You're nothing but a sewer, just like your boss."

I was furious at myself. I'd acted like a naïve jerk, but Ylenia had taken things too far and had broken a golden rule: if someone has you by the balls, you have to obey. Always. She'd pay dearly for that mistake.

Chapter Five
C'est lundi

Have you already spoken to Giuseppe Palamara?"

"Not yet," Tortorelli replied in a courteous tone. "I'd planned to do it Wednesday or Thursday."

I put on a grimace of disappointment. "Do you mind if I just skip work entirely this afternoon and tonight? I don't know how to explain it to you, but I can't seem to work the way I used to anymore. In fact, if you have any ideas about the menu, you should talk to the cook about it. My mind's a blank for some reason."

"Take your time, Pellegrini," he reassured me in a voice that sounded like a television pitchman. "La Nena is in good hands."

I parked my car close to Nicoletta's house. I took the rucksack with the handgun, the silencer, and other equipment that would be useful during the operation and I headed over, at a leisurely pace. I was early.

My ex partner wore her hair in a bun. That was new. The cigarette dangling from her lips was normal, though. "Where's the African?"

"Upstairs. He's getting dolled up."

I climbed the stairs and found him in front of the bathroom mirror, his face covered with lather. He was singing and he kept on singing even after I came in.

"Rock 'n' roll," I observed. He nodded with satisfaction.

C'est lundi
Dans mon lit
Il est onze heures

Mal au coeur
Mal dormi
Envie de pipi . . .

"You're in a good mood," I commented.

"Today my whole life may change."

"Sure, money and a passport, too . . . Where do you think you might go?"

"Back to Africa. Where? . . . That's just a detail."

I went back downstairs. Nicoletta was loading the dishwasher. "Your black guest thinks he's going back to Africa."

"Poor fool. He doesn't know how good you are at destroying other people's dreams."

"So now you like him?"

"A little," she answered, with a tinge of irony.

"Smoke another cigarette and behave yourself. Today's not the day to be a shit for brains."

With split-second punctuality Mikhail showed up, and Nicoletta retreated upstairs. "Here comes the Cossack cavalry," he joked as he set two suitcases on the table in the living room. One suitcase contained clothing, gloves, and ski masks. The other held cell phones, handcuffs, duct tape, and guns. Brand new guns, still in the original packaging. I opened one of the boxes and picked up a large powerful-looking semiautomatic handgun.

"Where do these come from?" I asked, trying to decipher the writing on the slide.

"Poland," the Russian replied. "It's a 9 mm pistol. Fifteen rounds in the clip."

I handed it to the Chadian. "You think you can handle this? You're going to be on the front line."

He held it properly and did all the things that I would expect from someone who'd been in combat. "Nice gun," he commented, aiming at a wall. "It demands respect."

I got changed in the ground floor bathroom. Cheap Chinese garments. Jacket and trousers, shoes and tie all in basic black. White dress shirt. I looked in the mirror.

I looked like one of Tarantino's reservoir dogs. Another touch of *confusion* for our Calabrian friends.

"*Les cagoules* . . . the ski masks, there's only two of them," Hissène pointed out when I came back.

"The plan calls for someone to remember a black guy," I explained.

He grimaced with chagrin. "Everyone will see my face."

"That's what I want. Remember, to us you all look alike and no one will ever be capable of identifying you. The important thing is not to leave fingerprints," I added, tossing him a pair of gloves.

The highway was jammed with traffic and construction delays. Mikhail was doing a skillful job of driving the Japanese SUV that he'd stolen in a discotheque parking lot. The owner, little more than a boy, was so wacked out on drugs that he just handed his car keys to Mikhail with a grin. The Chadian proved to be quite a conversationalist and struck up a lengthy and demanding discussion with Mikhail of Russia's role on the African continent. After a while I couldn't take any more. I had hoped to sit in back and relax but that proved impossible.

"Can't you guys just talk about normal armed-robber topics? You know, like women, sports, and money?"

They both broke out laughing and Mikhail tuned the radio to a station that broadcast only Italian music. "Is that better?"

The singer was certain that the sun was there for everyone. I was pretty sure that Tortorelli and the Palamaras got up this morning with the same set of beliefs. I put my iPod earbuds in. Grace Slick's voice exploded into my head, urging me on, singing: "*You have a power all your own . . .* "

The gray metallic Lexus sedan emerged from the car rental

offices at 7 P.M. on the dot. It pulled onto the highway we'd just taken to get here, and the whole way it never went slower than 70 mph. The Russian rode the accelerator with a heavy foot and we got to the service plaza near Brescia well ahead of him. I handed the African one of the cell phones with a Bluetooth headset. That was how we'd communicate.

A guy in a white Fiat Punto was already there. He was waiting in his car in the parking lot near the phone booths. Smoke and one end of a cell phone conversation wafted out of the car's open windows. It was the time of the evening for panini and fast food while drivers of semi trailers hurried to find the best parking spots to bed down for the night. A highway patrol squad car pulled up in front of the bar. Tired faces, an espresso and a quick piss, and then back in the car to devour the miles on their shift. The Calabrians had picked an ideal place and time. No one was paying attention to anyone else.

The Lexus swung into the parking area and slowly prowled across it, finally stopping in front of the closed roll-down door of the repair bay. The guy in the Fiat Punto got out, locked his car with his remote control, and strolled off at a leisurely pace. Mikhail had told us that the next thing he'd do would be to get into the Lexus, have a short chat with his partner, and then get out carrying a dark blue gym bag.

Hissène was too fast for him. He came from around the corner and pulled open the passenger-side door. "Start the engine," I heard him say in my headset.

The driver stayed cool. "You can put down the piece. My wallet's in the glove compartment."

In the meanwhile, the guy from the white Fiat Punto had seen the African get in; at first he stopped and looked around, but then he sped up his pace.

"Hurry up," I snarled into the cell phone, turning around to look at the Russian. With the age-old pretext of tying his shoe, he was busy jamming a knife blade into one of the Fiat Punto's tires.

"I know exactly who you are and what this car is carrying," the Chadian said. "If you don't get moving I'll shoot you."

The driver did as he was told without another word, and the Lexus moved slowly toward the exit, followed by Mikhail who had returned to the SUV. We drove past the driver of the Punto as he was running back to his car.

"Where are we going?" the driver asked.

"Back to Milan, to the car rental place," the African replied.

"What do you know about the car rental company?"

"Shut up and pull off at the next exit."

I heard a cell phone ring. It had to be the guy in the Punto who wanted to know what the fuck was going on. The Chadian switched off the driver's phone, as he'd been instructed.

"Look in the rearview mirror," the Chadian told him. "You see the SUV that's following us? They're friends of mine."

"More fucking niggers like you, is that what you mean?"

It was time to intervene. "Let me talk to him."

The African took the headset off his ear and inserted it into the Calabrian's ear. "I'd suggest you keep calm," I said in a relaxed voice. "Giuseppe Palamara wants to know who's stealing his money."

"What the fuck is going on here?" he shouted in exasperation.

"Maybe it's Nilo and maybe you're his accomplice."

He calmed down and drove wordlessly for a while. As I expected, he couldn't put the pieces together. Finally, he said the only thing he knew for sure: "You're just trying to fuck with my head."

"That's right," I admitted without hesitation. "But you'd better shut up and behave if you want to stay alive."

Hissène took back the headset. "Did you search him?" I asked.

"He's unarmed."

"Be careful. He's smart and he's dangerous."

Mikhail, who'd said nothing until then, shot me a few quizzical glances. "You're wondering why I decided to start naming names with that fucked-up Mafioso."

"Exactly. There are times when the less said the better."

"Sure, you're right, but tomorrow morning you're going to vanish with your bag of money, while I'm going to have to deal with the feral cunning and mistrust that have made these miserable Calabrians rich, powerful, and feared everywhere. If they figure this out I'm a dead man. I'm just trying to sow some *confusion*."

He snickered. "*Dezinformatsia*. And do you think you fooled the driver?"

"He's confused, he doesn't know what to think. And that's already a good thing, this early in the game."

The rest of the drive was an unbroken monologue from the Calabrian as he attempted to establish a contact. I listened to him carefully, doing my best to parse the nuances and details.

He continually called me "big man." He was obviously distraught but he clearly had a pair of balls. No matter how things turned out, he'd have to pay. The price could be death or it might be a one-way ticket back to his little Calabrian village. He obviously knew that perfectly well, because it was clear that he'd grown up on bread and 'Ndrangheta and was a longtime soldier. He proved it when he started opining about the pistol that Hissène was holding on him.

"Hey, big man, explain something to me: I've got a nigger with a handgun that I wouldn't expect to see around here. You're Italian, no doubt about that, but it strikes me that you're the only one . . . "

I broke my silence. "Tell him that if what he's saying turned out to be true then we'd have to eliminate him." Hissène repeated my words.

A bitter laugh came out of the Calabrian's mouth. I knew that laugh. It was the laugh of a killer who'd done the killing himself too many times not to know that he'd reached the end of the line. I wondered why he didn't just crash the car and kill himself along with the man who was threatening him. That would foil all our well-laid plans. Maybe he wanted to go out in style, or else a thin thread of hope kept him from being swept away by anger. No. That wasn't it. He was just a Mafioso without an ounce of imagination. Mafia procedures absolutely forbid any independent thinking, unless it's been vetted in advance by the local boss.

About fifty yards from the offices of the car rental company was a small supermarket with an empty parking lot behind it. The African told him to drive around back and showed him where to park the car.

"Turn off the engine and give me the keys," he ordered.

The man did as he was told and a bullet blew his kidney apart.

"Just like in the movies," the Russian commented when he saw the powder flash light up the interior of the Lexus for a fraction of a second.

We got out of the SUV and started ridding the Lexus of every single object we could find, while the Chadian took care of the dead man's personal effects. Perched on the rear seat of the Lexus were four identical bags. I opened one at random. Cash. For a second I was tempted to pull out my gun and eliminate both my accomplices. I'd done that once before and I knew nothing could be easier. Unfortunately, I still needed them. I looked up and my eyes met Mikhail's. He was watching me. I smiled at him. Might as well be straight with him. "I'll admit it, it did occur to me," I whispered.

"I know. But it's not worth trying to figure which of us has the faster draw. That usually winds up with both of us gut-shot on the pavement."

"Cossack wisdom?"

"Hollywood."

In three minutes flat we'd cleaned out the Lexus, leaving

nothing but a corpse with empty pockets. Another morsel of *confusion* for the Palamaras. I checked my watch. We were running behind schedule.

"Don't break the speed limit but do your best to make up some time," I told Mikhail.

I checked the dead man's wallet. His name was Zosimo Terreti and he'd shuffled off this mortal coil at the age of forty-nine.

I called Nicoletta, who according to our plan was supposed to spend the evening with Gemma at La Nena to keep an eye on Tortorelli. "How's it going?"

"He got a phone call and now he seems anxious. He keeps calling someone but gets no answer."

"Warn me if he leaves the restaurant."

I turned the Calabrian's cell phone back on. In a short time a cascade of messages came in from three unavailable callers. The contacts directory was empty and so was the queue of sent messages. Zosimo was a disciplined soldier.

The Russian and the African had done their jobs perfectly. As the mileage separating us from both the Veneto and the city diminished, a critical moment for our little gang was drawing closer: time to split up the take. I reached down and touched the silencer where it was taped to my leg. The gun had a bullet in the chamber.

My cell phone rang. It was Nicoletta. "We're leaving. We're the last customers."

I figured out the timeline. The waitstaff still had to clean up. What with one thing and another, Tortorelli would have to stay at La Nena for at least another hour. According to my original plan, I was supposed to wind up face-to-face with the bookkeeper but solo, after we'd split the take and said our farewells at Nicoletta's house. There wasn't time for that now.

"There's been a change in plans," I announced. "We're going

to have to swing by and pick up the bookkeeper after the little puppet show at the hotel. He'll help us count the money."

Mikhail and Hissène didn't blink an eye. I realized that by now the tension in the SUV was so dense you could slice it.

Mikhail parked a hundred feet or so from the front door of the Negresco Palace, where the bookkeeper had been staying. I handed Hissène a dark blue bag. He hopped out and vanished into the lobby. He was supposed to go up to the night clerk and ask for Tortorelli. When the clerk told him that Tortorelli hadn't come in yet the Chadian was to act annoyed and beat it fast. Just one more brainteaser for the Palamaras to try to figure out.

As soon as the Chadian got back in the car I used Zosimo Terreti's cell phone to text Tortorelli: "Appointment confirmed."

"You think he'll fall for it?" the Russian asked.

"I can't say," I answered. It depended on how deeply steeped in the 'Ndrangheta's culture the dickhead really was. The guy we killed in Milan would have seen it for what it was from a mile away, but the bookkeeper was a different matter. He was a technician, as he'd described himself. He was exactly the kind of trained personnel that the 'Ndrangheta needed in order to modernize, but which the various crime families hadn't yet had time to develop from within the ranks. Probably the initial contact had been through the loansharking operation that had stripped him of his company and had turned him into an employee of the Calabrians.

When we pulled into Piazza Vittoria di Lepanto he was already there, waiting for his fellow Mafioso Zosimo. His eyes were scanning traffic for a metallic gray Lexus, and he only noticed the SUV when it pulled up beside him. I swung open the rear passenger door.

"Hop in," I said, showing him the dark blue gym bag. "We'll drive you to the hotel."

"How do you fit in?"

"I'll explain while we drive."

His eyes flickered forward to the front seats. He took in Mikhail and Hissène. He shook his head with determination. "I'm not getting in."

"Then I'll kill you," I threatened him, extending the pistol.

"Do you have any idea of who the Palamaras are?" he mumbled in fear.

"That's exactly why you should get in the car."

His legs were trembling and I had to help him in. His Eighties-era face was deformed by a grimace of terror.

"What happened to Signor Terreti?"

"He had a bad case of saturnism," I replied. "He couldn't come."

Mikhail broke in, asking what I'd just said. I explained: "It's another word for lead poisoning."

The Russian and the Chadian both burst out laughing. The bookkeeper took my hand. Delicately. As if I was his parish priest. "You don't know what they're like. I had to divorce my wife and leave my children to save their lives."

"So you decided to come bust the balls of yours truly, who never did a thing to you?"

"I was just obeying orders."

"Bullshit! They'd already decided to kill me, hadn't they?"

"It was going to be a car crash," he admitted. "Right after you sold us La Nena."

"And you kept treating me like shit even though you knew they were going to kill me?"

"You're just so obnoxious that it came naturally to me," he answered frankly.

I couldn't believe my ears. I put a hand on his shoulder. "All right, Tortorelli. Now just behave and keep quiet. We have a ways to go."

The SUV left the city, followed a stretch of state route, then started climbing gentle slopes along twisting narrow roads.

Mikhail knew exactly where to go and after forty minutes or so turned off onto a dirt lane. The powerful headlights lit up orderly rows of grapevines.

"Where are we?" asked the bookkeeper.

"Everything you see belongs to Brianese," I answered. "Downhill from here he's building a fabulous villa."

The Russian turned off the engine but not the headlights. "We're here," he announced.

I shoved Tortorelli out of the SUV and threw an arm around his shoulders. "Just think what a lucky guy you are. You love wine, and you're going to spend eternity in a beautiful vineyard."

He fell to his knees. I reached into my backpack and pulled out a *prestige cuvée* champagne bottle. "You remember this?" I asked. "You drank one to my health."

"Cut it short," the Russian warned me.

I listened carefully and caught the distant barking of a dog. It wouldn't take long before the others joined in a nice canine chorus.

"You're right. But you have no idea how this asshole tortured me."

The bookkeeper started whining and I hit him over the head. He collapsed to the ground after the fourth blow from the bottle.

"Is he dead?" asked Mikhail.

"I have no idea. Let's bury him and if necessary I'll just finish him off with the shovel."

We dragged the body a few dozen yards along the slope. "This is the place," said the Cossack.

"Where's the girl?"

"Right next to him."

I congratulated myself for my farsighted brilliance in ordering Mikhail to bury Isabel on Brianese's estate. One day this could become a serious embarrassment for the Counselor.

Especially now that it was turning into quite the little cemetery.

I started to dig. The Chadian stuck a cigarette into his mouth but when he flicked his lighter the Russian stopped him. "Didn't you notice that I haven't smoked a cigarette all day? You leave your DNA on the cigarette butt and that just makes it easier for the cops."

The African mumbled an apology and skipped his cigarette.

"I can't do this anymore," I announced, dropping the shovel. "Hissène, you take a turn."

He bent down to pick up the shovel and went on with the digging. I sat down in the dark and wiped my face with the sleeve of my jacket.

"It's getting hot," I tossed out. It wasn't, actually, but I had to drown out the noise of the duct tape peeling away from my leg so that I could remove the silencer. As I chatted with Mikhail about how spring and fall were disappearing as seasons because of global warming, I managed to screw the tube onto the pistol, flip off the safety, and get off two shots into the Chadian's body. I'd hit him in the back. He wasn't dead and he was panting heavily, trying to get out a few words.

I waved the pistol in the air to empty the hot fumes out of the silencer. I stepped over and fired a final shot right behind his ear.

"I'm willing to bet you've got the drop on me," I murmured to the Russian who was behind me.

"It's nothing but a precaution, my friend. Now, I wouldn't mind pulling the trigger, but my gun would make too much noise and there are only two roads out of here."

"We should find a solution. This is starting to wear on me."

"Let's throw away our weapons and search each other before we split up the money."

"That sounds like a good idea."

I laid the pistol with the silencer on the ground and went

back to digging. A good yard deep for a double grave. Tortorelli was on the bottom, with his arms wrapped around the bottle of champagne that had killed him, with the African on top of him. We scattered a kilo of pepper over the bodies and filled the grave back up with dirt.

On our way back to the city we stopped at a bend in the river and got rid of our weapons and the cell phones we'd used in the robbery. We searched each other thoroughly, then I insisted on going over the interior of the SUV with a fine-toothed comb. I tossed everything into the water that could cut you or hit you over the head.

"All right," I said with satisfaction. "Now I'm going to give you your share."

"What the African was supposed to get and a little extra," he specified. "We never said anything about me helping to take care of Tortorelli."

Each duffel bag contained 250,000 euros. Four bags made a million. The 'Ndrangheta that had taken root in Lombardy, and which the Palamaras belonged to, had been forced to turn to the Veneto under pressure from a police investigation and was laundering four million euros a month there. Not bad.

I dropped the Russian off at an intersection on the outskirts of the city. In my rearview mirror I saw him freeing a bicycle from the chain that secured it to a metal fence and pedaling off with 400,000 euros stuffed into a duffel bag. It didn't make me feel happy to know that he was still alive, and not so much because of the money, which was certainly a substantial sum, but because you just never know. People have the bad habit of doing fucked up things like emerging out of the past, and maybe showing up years later to ask a favor. Mikhail was a die-hard and the only way of killing him would have have been a gunfight at close range. Experience taught me, however, that ever since the times of Johnny Ringo, gunfights were a very good way of catching a bullet in the gut.

I went straight to Nicoletta's house and parked in the courtyard. The sun was already well over the horizon and I wanted to make an effort to get into La Nena at a decent hour. Cigarette trailing a stream of smoke, breath reeking of alcohol, face drawn with weariness and tension, Nicoletta seemed to have aged overnight.

She pointed to the dirt on my shoes and clothing. "A little nocturnal gardening?"

I pulled a hundred thousand euros out of the bag and slammed it down on the table. "Today you're going to call a moving service and get everything out of this house. You have forty-eight hours to get out of town."

"Don't worry," she said. "I've got it all organized."

"Good. Now go to your bedroom. I've got things to do." She stood up.

"Lock the door when you leave."

I changed my clothes and I examined every scrap of paper and object that we'd taken out of the Lexus and the Calabrian's pockets. There was nothing that could be useful to me in dealing with the second part of the plan. That was going to be the really hard part, with the 'Ndrangheta investigating and me as one of the prime suspects. I wrapped everything up together and stuck the other 500,000 euros into my backpack. Last of all I mixed up a concoction of cough lozenges made up of potassium chlorate and confectioner's sugar and I put it into a plastic receptacle. I made a hole in the cap and inserted a cigarette with the filter snapped off. I put it under the back seat of the SUV, where the Russian had already placed a five-liter gas can. I'd learned to make rudimentary bombs in the Seventies, when I had talked myself into believing I was a revolutionary, and I was still pretty good at it.

Mingling with morning traffic I drove the SUV to the other side of town, near an abandoned factory that had been occupied by young activists from a community center, detested equally by the city administration and the police. I lit the cigarette and walked off with the backpack slung over my shoulder, wearing a visored cap and sunglasses. Exactly three minutes later I reached the terminus of a bus line that was scheduled to leave before the bomb went off. I got off at the stop for the train station, hopped into a cab, and told the driver to drop me off near where I'd parked my car.

At the first red light I called Martina.

She picked up on the first ring. "Ciao, darling, how are you?"

I turned around and looked at the half million euros sitting on the back seat. "Great. And your father? How's his treatment going?" I asked, pretending to be deeply concerned.

I missed my wife. I needed an extended session of sex. I'd committed an armed robbery and a couple of murders. Creative criminality had triggered an insane lust for life and pleasure. I couldn't restrain myself. I called Gemma.

"Ciao, King of Hearts," she whispered. "I'm at work, so I can't talk about the filthy things you make me do."

"Too bad. It would have helped me to hold out until this evening."

"Do you have bad intentions, King of Hearts?"

"Very bad intentions."

At La Nena, I asked everyone if they'd seen Tortorelli. I acted the part of the astonished dupe until it was obvious to everyone that that's what I was. I searched through every drawer that the bookkeeper had stuck his hands into. As I suspected, I found absolutely nothing that might be of any use. At last, I went back to managing my restaurant. My first official act was to eject a vendor of somersaulting light-up monkey toys.

"Get the hell out of here," I said in a loud voice. That was greeted with a sprinkling of applause from the diners.

I told the youngest waiter to go get Ding Dong and tell him to come back to work.

After lunch I told my trusted waiter Piero that I'd be back in midafternoon and asked him to call me if the bookkeeper showed up.

"Do you have an appointment?" asked the secretary.

"No."

"Just who are you? A supplier, a client, a representative?"

"A dear friend of Signora Marenzi's husband."

"What did you say your name was?"

"Pellegrini. Giorgio Pellegrini."

The receptionist got up from her desk at the front of the large open space offices and went off in search of her boss. I had heard that Brianese's wife continued to run her fashion company just to stave off boredom. From what I could see here, that was just another typical small-town rumor prompted by jealous minds. Everywhere I looked, young people were busy discussing, designing, and creating. The actual apparel was produced in China, but it was unmistakable that the woman who ran this place was an old-school entrepreneur of northeastern Italy. Excellent. That would make it easier to come to an agreement.

The secretary came hurrying back and handed me a cordless phone.

"I know who you are, Signor Pellegrini," Signora Marenzi's voice launched into me. "I don't believe you're one of Sante's friends at all. In fact, it's not my understanding that my husband even frequents your establishment anymore."

"We've had our disagreements recently, it's true. And it's true that he no longer honors my restaurant with his patronage," I admitted in a conciliatory tone. "But you really don't know who I am. Believe me when I tell you that you're all wrong about me."

"Get out of here."

"Whatever you say, but the merchandise I possess is negotiable elsewhere."

She snorted. "You don't think you can bleed money out of me with some local two-bit scandal, do you?"

"I think no such thing. But this isn't about a little blot of mud that can be hidden away by ignoring it, the way your husband's colleagues usually do."

"Why don't you approach him directly?"

"Because you're the only one who can give me what I want."

She hung up and a few minutes later she emerged from the design department. She had to be at least sixty but she looked ten years younger and when she was a young woman she must have been a knockout. She waved me into her office. It was filled with objects of all kinds, swaths and rolls of fabric, and patterns. She pointed me to a chair across from her desk.

"We ordinary mortals who have to work for a living, instead of blackmailing our fellow man, usually don't have a lot of time to waste."

I explained what was at stake and what I wanted from her. She had an intriguing way of running her fingers over her face when she was thinking.

"Part of me says I should just ask you: 'Is that all?' and then I would be rid of you, but the matter would become uncontrollable if this information became public."

"That's not going to happen. It's not in anybody's interest," I reassured her.

"All right then. I accept your terms."

I stood up and pulled a large bunch of keys out of my jacket pocket and set them down in front of her.

She picked up the keys as if she'd found them in a pool of manure and dropped them into a drawer. "You've ruined my day, Signor Pellegrini."

What a woman. I turned on my heel and left.

Chapter six
Ombretta

They showed up Wednesday morning. Two days after the disappearance of Tortorelli, Terreti, and a million euros. I recognized them immediately. One of the pair was the guy in the white Fiat Punto who we'd blindsided at the service plaza. The other guy was a character with a peasant face and a cruel manner. They showed up for breakfast, lunch, and dinner, and they never missed an aperitif. They sat in watchful, attentive silence. Apparently I was the only person or object in which they showed no interest whatever. At first the waitstaff took them for cops. Then they figured out these guys must be on the other side of the law and they simply ignored them entirely. When I went to take orders at their table they kept their eyes glued to their menus.

On Friday they started shadowing me. The following Monday they disappeared. As if they'd never existed. They didn't reappear until that night. At Gemma's apartment.

The guy from the white Fiat Punto came to open the door. I feigned surprise and fear and he jerked his head wearily, signaling me inside.

In the living room, Giuseppe and Nilo Palamara were waiting for me. The guy with the face of a peasant must have been in the other room with Gemma. I went on acting.

"What are you doing here? Where's my friend?"

"Sit down," ordered Nilo.

I obeyed. It wasn't hard for me to display all the terror that was twisting my bowels. The two Palamaras stared at me for a long time with ostentatiously threatening expressions. Then Nilo went around to stand behind me. A typical cop move, a signal that my interrogation was about to begin. In fact, Giuseppe broke the silence.

"There's a thing that happened. No matter how we look at it, from below, above, from right or left . . . everything points to you."

"I don't know what you're talking about."

Nilo gave me a glancing slap. "Uncle Giuseppe's not done talking."

"Pardon," I hastened to apologize.

"Somebody put on a puppet show with people appearing and disappearing and all done special to pull the wool over our eyes. There was even an African in a jacket and tie."

"An African?"

Nilo grabbed me by the hair and yanked so it hurt. "That's right, an African," he breathed into my face. "A friend of yours."

"You've got this all wrong."

Uncle Giuseppe waved his index finger. "No. You're up to your neck in this puppet show," he said. "Maybe you didn't direct the show because you're too stupid, but you definitely were one of the puppets. Here's why."

He lifted his thumb: "First of all, Monday you didn't go to work."

Then he lifted his index finger: "Bookkeeper Tortorelli disappeared that same night."

Last of all, his middle finger, outspread: "Tuesday morning an SUV was burned the way people burn cars when all evidence needs to be destroyed because the car was used to do something wrong."

"Tortorelli, an SUV . . . Signor Palamara, could you explain things a little more clearly? Because I don't know what you're talking about."

Nilo hit me again. Harder and meaner this time. "Don't waste our time with this little game of asking us to tell you things you already know."

Giuseppe raised a hand to stop his nephew. "Listen, Pellegrini, your friend is tied up like a salami on the kitchen table in there. And you know what you do with a salami, right? You slice it up. Is that clear?"

"Have you lost your minds? She has nothing to do with any of this and neither do I. Leave us alone!"

Palamara snickered. "I bet you were with her Monday night."

"No. I was with a woman but it wasn't Gemma."

"Who was she?"

"I can't tell you that. She's a married woman, and if her husband ever finds out I'll never hear the end of it."

"That's what they all say," he muttered in disappointment. He turned to his nephew.

"Go tell our friend to start with the nose."

"All right, all right," I practically shouted. "I was with Brianese's wife."

An icy silence descended. Giuseppe looked at me and reflected. I twisted and turned in my chair, muttering meaningless phrases like an innocent but terrified man. I wasn't actually afraid anymore. In fact, the adrenaline of victory was sizzling in my veins. Those stupid Mafiosi had underestimated me. They'd fucked it up for themselves by adopting a standard procedure.

"But she's old," he commented after a while. "Is there something wrong with you, Pellegrini? Why don't you have sex with women your age, like any ordinary Christian?"

"She doesn't look her age," I explained. "And she makes love like a twenty-year-old."

"Where did you two spend the night?"

I promptly supplied the addess of the residential hotel where Ylenia and the Counselor had their love nest.

"How late did you stay together?"

"I didn't leave until eight the next morning. I think Ombretta left half an hour later."

Uncle and nephew exchanged a glance. Giuseppe pulled out his cell phone and moved into the bedroom. "Hello, Sante, sorry to call at this time of night . . . " I heard him say, but then he closed the door.

Fifteen minutes later we were driving across town, heading for the Counselor's apartment. I was sitting in the backseat, wedged between the two thugs. The Palamaras were sitting in front and muttering in thick dialect.

Brianese was pale and worried when he let us in. "What's going on? At this time of night, at my home . . . " Then he saw me and froze. "What the hell is he doing here?"

Giuseppe grabbed his arm to attract his attention. "We need to speak to your wife, tell her to come downstairs."

"That's completely out of the question," he hissed. "Come see me tomorrow morning in my law office and you can explain what you want at leisure, but Ombretta stays out of this."

Palamara gripped his arm even tighter and the Counselor tried in vain to break free. "This is an important matter for us," Giuseppe explained. "Important and urgent. Tell her to come downstairs now. Otherwise I'm going to have to send one of my boys upstairs and she'll have an unpleasant awakening, with a stranger in her bedroom."

It became clear to Brianese that his being a prominent lawyer, not to mention a member of the Italian parliament, the fact that he was in his own home, these things meant less than nothing because the Calabrians simply didn't give a damn. They wanted something, and they were going to get it.

"Wait here for a minute," he said, heading upstairs, his shoulders sagging in defeat.

A few minutes later, Ombretta Brianese née Marenzi strode

downstairs briskly, followed by her husband. She was wearing an extremely elegant purple silk dressing gown and a pair of Friulian velvet slippers in the same color.

She threw everyone off balance by shaking hands all around and introducing herself. When it was my turn she caressed my cheek fleetingly, and greeted me by name: "Ciao, Giorgio."

"You know him?" the Counselor stammered.

Giuseppe Palamara interrupted by coming straight to the point. "Forgive me, Signora, but I absolutely have to know whether you spent Monday night with Giorgio Pellegrini."

"The answer is no," Brianese butted in, increasingly aghast. "You can go now."

"He asked your wife," Nilo hushed him.

"Let me see if I understand this," Ombretta began, as if she were upbraiding an incompetent parking valet. "You bust into my house at four in the morning demanding to know intimate details concerning my private life? Who the hell do you think you are? I doubt that you're from the police because you don't have the look. We may well be in Italy, where there's no longer any respect for personal privacy, but I think even the police would deal with these things in a manner more in keeping with such a delicate topic . . . "

"Answer him, goddamn it!" shouted her husband in exasperation.

Signora Marenzi looked Giuseppe Palamara right in the eye. "Yes, we were together until eight in the morning. We meet in a residential hotel, located in Via Martiri delle Foibe, no. 8. Or rather, I should say, we used to meet, because after tonight's unexpected development good taste requires that we put an end to our relationship."

She turned around, picked up her purse from an armchair, and pulled out a bunch of keys that she handed over to the Calabrian. "Don't pay the slightest attention to the furnishings; they're in terrible taste but they're perfectly suited to the purpose of the apartment," she said, before turning and going back upstairs.

I peeked over at Brianese. He was frozen solid with shock. The picture of a man in ruins. And his reaction was so unmistakably sincere that the Calabrians could hardly miss it. Even if his wife and I were both excellent actors, there were good reasons to suspect that both yours truly and the lady of the house might well be pulling the wool over their eyes. Not the Counselor. He was the very picture of sincerity.

Palamara handed back the keys, turned and headed for the door. They were kind enough to drive me back to Gemma's apartment. Giuseppe turned around suddenly and shot me a look. "Still, you must have had something to do with it."

That wasn't what I'd expected to hear. He would brood over that suspicion endlessly and if he couldn't figure out a plausible alternative, then he'd start up with me again. It wasn't over with the Calabrians yet, but I wasn't worried. I had faith in the resources of creative criminality.

Gemma was stretched out and tied to the kitchen table. I took the gag and blindfold off her.

"King of Hearts," she stuttered. "I don't like this game."

I kissed her on the lips and started taking off my clothes. "Now I'll take over, baby, and you'll see I'll drive you crazy."

My cell phone rang while I was slipping her panties down her legs. It was Brianese. "Come to my law office tomorrow morning."

"No. The back room is more secure and it's been a while since you've shown your face around La Nena. I'll expect you for an aperitif."

"So you want to humiliate me right up to the end, don't you?"

"Sure," I said, and then I hung up.

At the end of a dull day, the lawyer and member of the

Italian parliament Sante Brianese walked into my restaurant with his usual determined step. He behaved like the consummate actor he was and looked like the happiest man in the world. He shook hands and slapped backs, reeling off wisecracks, ancedotes, and jokes. Finally, he walked into the back room and I followed with a tray of cold cuts and vegetables preserved in oil and a bottle of white wine, the way he liked it.

He ate and drank frantically, the way he did when his stress was out of control. Every so often we exchanged a glance. He didn't really know how to get started or what to say. Events had overwhelmed him. Things had hurtled far out of control. The great thing was that there were still so many things he didn't know about, like Ylenia's betrayal.

I decided to turn the tables. "It's no fun having the 'Ndrangheta in your house, is it, Counselor?" I said. "Once they get their foot in the door it's hard to get rid of them. You need to act smart and be absolutely pitiless and fearless."

"You dragged my wife into this mess, you son of a bitch," he hissed furiously. "I don't know what really happened, but if you think you're going to dupe Giuseppe Palamara, you're just an unfortunate fool."

I grabbed him by the lapel of his jacket and pulled his ear close to my mouth. "I didn't do a thing, but if, just to speculate, I really had arranged for Bookkeeper Tortorelli's disappearance, I can assure you that I'd bury him somewhere on your estate, Counselor. That way, I could confess to that asshole Giuseppe that I'd done it at your orders. It wouldn't save my life, but it would ensure that your life and the lives of your wife and daughters wouldn't be worth shit anymore."

I released him. He leapt to his feet. "What the hell are you? You're a monster."

I took offense at that one and I hauled off and slapped him, not very hard, but deeply humiliating for a bigwig like him.

"I'm the biggest, baddest wolf of all, Counselor. It's a good thing I'm your friend."

"What do you want?"

I extended my arms and gripped him by the shoulders. I carefully lowered him into his chair. "I want the Calabrians to stop busting my balls once and for all. Also, I want La Nena to go back to being your favorite restaurant, and last of all, I want the two-and-a-quarter million euros that you owe me. You can pay in installments. I'm in no hurry."

I poured him some wine and he threw it back in a single gulp. He sighed. "I don't know what to do about the Palamaras. There's a fellow member of parliament involved and other party leaders in Lombardy— "

"Don't worry about that. Mafiosi never mention politicians' names, at least until they turn state's witnesses," I said, crunching my teeth down on a breadstick. "I can direct you to a deputy commissioner of police who's got his hands dirty with a prostitution ring. He could steer certain choice morsels of information to his colleagues in Milan . . . he'd come out of it with a nice glow and you'd be kept out of it entirely."

He stood up. "Okay. What's his name?"

I told him. He carefully wiped his mouth with his napkin and then filled it with hard mints. He started sucking on the mints pensively. "How did you manage to track down the residential hotel and how did you get a copy of the keys?" he suddenly asked.

I put on an expression of pure astonishment. "I had nothing to do with it. That was your wife's doing."

"I don't believe that you slept with Ombretta."

"What does your Signora say?"

"That it's true," he replied, glaring a challenge at me.

That Signora Marenzi was quite some woman. "Oh, it's true, Counselor. You are one spectacular cuckold," I said in a jocular tone, imitating the voice of Italy's prime minister.

He shot me a glance of scorching fury. I held out both arms apologetically. "Do you remember that time, in fact it was right here in the back room, after you sold me off to the Palamaras, that you said: 'Giorgio, you can't imagine how happy I am right now?'" I asked in an exaggeratedly pained tone of voice. "Well, now it's my turn so I hope you don't take it the wrong way if I have my little joke."

I smoothed his jacket lapel and walked him to the door. He was a cuckold of legendary proportions and a complete piece of shit. I'd just told him that there was a corpse fertilizing his vineyard and all he cared about was whether or not I'd fucked his wife. That got me thinking; I understood that my dealings with my friend Sante were not over.

CHAPTER SEVEN
Man at Work

Palamara's thugs kept showing up at my restaurant. Every so often they'd drop by to eat lunch or drink a glass of something. I unfailingly treated them with exquisite and fearful courtesy, never forgetting to send my best wishes to Signor Giuseppe and to Signor Nilo. The real problem was Gemma, who recognized them one evening and went over the edge into something approaching a nervous breakdown. I was forced to take her home and give her a triple dose of Xanax.

One day Giuseppe dropped by in person. He ate heartily and invited me to sit down and help him polish off a bottle of a 2006 Solaia. "Have you put your ring of whores back together?" he asked, after extending his compliments to the chef.

"No, and I'm not going to."

"Just who was it that used to procure the girls for you?"

I'd been waiting for that question for a while. "From an escort service. As you know all too well, there's an embarass-ment of riches."

He flashed me a smile of reproof. "You're trying to pull the fucking wool over my eyes."

"That's true," I admitted. "But I don't have anything to do with your problems. If you haven't set your heart at rest about that it just means you've got too much time on your hands."

He stuck his nose deep into his glass and pretended to be lost in the inebriating perfume of that full-bodied red. "It's not smart to talk to me like that."

"It wasn't my idea to bring Tortorelli around here and if he took off with your money I certainly didn't help him."

"Is that what you think?"

"It's what I've been able to come up with given the scanty information available to me."

"The bookkeeper would never have skipped out of his own free will, Pellegrini. Somebody helped him," he retorted confidently.

"Well, why should that have been me?"

He laid his finger alongside his nose. "Because you reek."

"What do I reek of?"

"It's a sort of sickly sweet odor. The smell of flowers, or dead men."

"Well, let me thank you for that glass of wine and the interesting conversation, Signor Palamara. But I'd better go tend to my customers."

"Go on, go right ahead. We'll be seeing more of each other."

He left without paying, as if La Nena were his personal property. He'd dropped by to let me know me that he'd figured it out: I'd organized the knockover with the same gang of people that supplied me with prostitutes. He'd come to that conclusion by ruling out all other possibilities and now he was certain of it. Let a little more time go by and he'd track down Mikhail Sholokhov, but he'd be able to identify Nicoletta in less time than that. I tried calling her to warn her, but the number was no longer in service. After all, I had told her she'd better disappear.

I complained to Brianese about the way the Calabrian boss was still on my case, but he wasn't particularly helpful. As far as he knew, the investigation was being slow-tracked and it would be several months before the magistrates were ready to sign arrest warrants.

The Counselor showed that he'd learned his lesson and he did everything possible to bring the old clientele back to La

Nena. He'd come in with Ylenia and with Nicola, his personal assistant, and everything seemed to have gone back to normal.

I decided I could tell Martina to come home. Her father's health hadn't improved, but it had been a useful exercise from many points of view and it had made things easier for her sisters for a good long period of time.

The night before she returned I talked to Gemma and spelled things out clearly. "Martina is my wife and you're just my lover; you can be replaced in five minutes."

"I'll be a very good girl, King of Hearts," she promised in a piping toddler's voice.

Later that night, while I was watching an episode of my favorite television show, *Justified*, and absentmindedly fondling Gemma's tits, I asked her if she'd heard from Nicoletta. She told me she hadn't seen her or heard from her in a while.

The next morning I swung by my ex-partner's little villa. The front door and the windows were wide open and there were a couple of painters working in the front hallway. I stopped and asked whether the house was for sale. They weren't Italian and showed no signs of wanting to talk to me. I pulled out twenty euros and offered to trade it for the phone number of whoever had hired them. In authentic Veneto dialect the painter told me that the house had already been sold and that they'd been hired by the new owner.

I organized a little party at La Nena to celebrate my darling's return home. I hired a duo, guitarist and vocalist, who specialized in covers of songs by Lucio Battisti.

Martina came straight to the restaurant from the train station and when she walked in the musicians began playing *The Man Who Loves You.*

Oh! Woman you are mine,
And when I say mine

I mean you're not leaving:
You'd better stay here
And make love in my bed!

It was an excellent return on 200 euros. She was deeply moved, she ran across the room and threw herself into my arms in front of the roomful of customers. They burst into applause and were sufficiently supportive to deserve a round of prosecco on the house.

I had lots of work to take care of so I couldn't spend more than a few minutes with her. Gemma looked after her and made sure that Martina was comfortable and relaxed. I'd told Gemma to ask Martina lots of questions about her experiences in Germany, so that she'd already be sick of talking about it by the time she got home.

She was waiting for me in the bathroom for the ritual of creams and ointments, which I'd really been missing. She started touching herself but stopped almost immediately. "Please, I want you to take over."

I went over to where she stood by the sink and satisfied her request. Then I took her to bed where we made love for a long time and fell asleep with our arms wrapped around each other.

After breakfast she talked to me for exactly half an hour, about her father, the clinic, and her life in Lahnstein with her mother. I noticed that she was a good storyteller. She knew how to put a listener at ease.

Then she spoiled it all while I was leaving for work. "I can see you almost never slept here."

"So?"

"When I was all alone in Germany I sensed that you were with another woman."

I took her chin in my hand. "I don't want to talk about it. It's been a tough period."

"It has been for a while now, Giorgio."

"In fact, tonight I'm going to need all your devotion. Can I count on that?"

"You know you can."

According to my calculations, Brianese must be in Rome and that reckoning was confirmed when I saw Ylenia come into the restaurant alone. The last thing she wanted to do was drop by La Nena for an aperitif but she had no choice. I greeted her with the usual kiss on the cheek and told her to come join me in the back room.

"I urgently need to get in touch with Nicoletta Rizzardi to warn her about a certain situation . . . "

"Have you lost her phone number?"

"It's no longer in service and she must be out of town. I want you to get in touch with her brother for me."

"Is that all?"

I didn't need anything else but she'd been bitchy enough that it was always useful to remind her that I was the last person on earth that she could afford to disrespect.

"No," I answered rudely. "Have you moved your little love nest yet?"

"We will soon."

"Ombretta didn't like the interior decoration."

"So I heard."

"You want to know something else, Ylenia? You're not worth that woman's little finger."

"She's such a magnificent woman that she can do anything she sets her mind to, except make a man happy. And that's something I'm very good at."

"He put these ridiculous ideas in your head, didn't he?"

She ignored me. She had something else she wanted to tell me. "I'll hate you for the rest of my life for what you've done."

"Hatred is a dangerous beast. Keep it on a leash. It can make you do things you'll live to regret," I advised her in a neutral tone. "Sex is the best therapy." And I doubled down on the details about the Counselor's sexual predilections that she'd unwisely confided to me. Once she was crying hard enough to make her mascara run, I let her go.

When I got back to the bar I noticed one of the Calabrian thugs sipping a Campari. Giuseppe Palamara wasn't giving up. I picked up my cell phone and called Roby De Palma.

"I haven't seen you in a while," I said. The background noise suggested he was in a crowded restaurant. "I've heard that you've put down roots at Alfio's place, where the Padanos meet to eat, but I don't want you to forget that the food is better at my place."

"Do you miss me or do you have some work for me?" he asked in a pragmatic tone of voice.

"A little of both. I miss you, so I'll treat you to dinner. I have some work for you, and that involves a nice wad of crisp new bills."

I sensed a moment's hesitation so I hastened to reassure him. "Nothing weird or tricky. Pure routine."

He relaxed. "Is there a table available?"

"For you? Always."

In the time it took to leave Alfio's and walk across a few piazzas in the center of the city, the private investigator walked through the front door of La Nena. A few customers playfully jeered him for the traitor he was and he shot back mockingly that they were just sore about the tanning they'd taken at the polls and embarrassed by the intemperate, ridiculous, and risqué outbursts of the prime minister.

I let him stuff himself and guzzle like a king until dessert. Then I sat down at his table. He pointed to the table where Martina and Gemma were sitting.

"Storm warnings in your family?" he asked. "You haven't looked at her once since she walked in the place."

I snorted. "I love her to death but she is such a pain in the ass."

"Like every woman on earth," he said brusquely and

changed the subject. "This was a first rate dinner, I have to say, but it won't get you a special rate. What can I do for you?"

I uttered a name. Nothing more.

"Well, it's a good thing it's just a routine assignment," he commented in a worried voice.

"It is, don't work yourself up. All I need is for you find a contact who can arrange for me to transmit a message to him in an absolutely secure way. This has nothing to do with politics or even Italy. It has to do with a foreign business opportunity for which I'd get a percentage."

He caught a whiff of money and his scruples diminished. "How much are you offering? I can't go by my hourly rate on something like this."

"Ten thousand."

We shook hands. "Give me a couple of days."

I looked up and my eyes met the gaze of the Calabrian, who was watching us curiously. I had no doubt that when the private investigator left the restaurant Giuseppe Palamara's thug would follow him. I went over to Ding Dong and discreetly slipped him a hundred euros. "What do you want me to do, boss?"

"Beat up a guy."

"Who?"

I pointed to him. "Wait until he gets away from here."

"But he's white!"

"He's white but he's done some bad things. I don't want him to set foot in La Nena again."

"I'm on it, boss."

When Roby De Palma came over to the counter to say goodbye, the Calabrian slipped out the door. After a short while Ding Dong came back in and gave me a wink. A few longtime customers walked in and came over to the counter, complaining that my bouncer had beaten down an apparently innocent passerby for no good reason. I treated them to a round of drinks and explained that the guy that had caught the beating was a pusher and that he'd been spotted repeatedly loitering outside a high school that was only a few hundred yars away from the restaurant.

"Then he treated him too gently," complained one of the customers. "He should have broken his legs. They're easier to spot if they're limping."

"Spinning, baby, spinning," I ordered in a loud voice, as I shut the front door of our apartment. Martina emerged from the darkness. She was nude. She took both my hands and held them up to her lips.

After she fell into a deep and restorative slumber, from which she wouldn't awaken until her metabolism had recovered, I got up and went into my office. There I edited the video of Ylenia's confession into a reliable and marketable product. I created a short audio extract that could prove useful as a first sample.

They waited until I showed up at La Nena. Then they went over to Ding Dong. One of them asked him something and the other stabbed him three times in the belly in quick succession. Typical prison technique. Arm bent upward; short, sharp thrusts. The bouncer walked in from the sidewalk, pressing his hands against the stab wounds. I told him to lay down and told a waiter to get a tablecloth and apply it to stop the hemorrhaging.

The doctor at the emergency room told me Ding Dong was in pretty bad shape and that he was sending him directly into surgery. I called Ding Dong's mother and then went back to work. I told the police that last night Ding Dong had chased away someone he assumed was a drug dealer. A Maghrebi or a Romanian, I couldn't remember exactly. While I was talking to the cops one of Palamara's men came in. It was probably one of the guys who'd attacked Ding Dong. He stood at the bar not six feet away and ordered a Fernet Branca. I didn't give a fuck about my bouncer. I'd only used him to make sure that they couldn't follow and identify Roby De Palma, but the Palamaras were starting to take things a little too far.

Then it was my turn to be questioned by reporters. They asked me to pose on the scene of the attack and focused on the bloodstained cobblestones, while I repeated my fairytale about the drug dealer, calling on the public authorities and the police to make sure that the center of town became a safe place for honest citizens again.

In midafternoon the procession of security experts looking for work began. I asked each man one question: "Ever been in jail?"

I hired the only applicant who'd been willing to admit he had and to specify the crime and the time served. The restaurant was suddenly more crowded and profitable than ever. When the doctors reported that Ding Dong was going to pull through I announced it live and Ylenia proposed a toast to a brave man who had risked his life to keep the drug dealers out of our neighborhood. I slipped a thousand euros into an envelope and sent it Ding Dong's mother. The 'Ndrangheta thug was the last customer to leave the restaurant.

I'd made up my mind to go see Gemma, but Martina called me when I was halfway there. "You need my complete devotion again tonight. I'm ready for you."

I put up resistance and ventured onto the territory of absolute power: I forced her to dig deep into her most hidden fantasies to see if she could come up with something that would make me want to go back to her. She managed to electrify me.

"I'm benching you for the night," I told Gemma.

"Oh, King of Hearts, I'll be so brokenhearted."

There are powerful men like Sante Brianese. There are others like Giuseppe Palamara. The one I wanted to contact didn't fit into any clearly defined category. He'd inherited his power and he'd managed to preserve and use it with great skill, nimbly sidestepping the great tidal waves of scandals that had decimated the Italian ruling class. He'd judiciously measured out his own media exposure. Unlike so many others, he made appearances only when he had something important to say, and he always did so with excellent manners and great respect. He'd constructed a reputation as a gentleman at home in the countryside, even though he had homes scattered around the financial capitals of the world, and he'd been one of the first manufacturers to move the family industry offshore, to Romania. He'd never concealed his right-leaning political sympathies but he'd always refused to be lured into pursuing public office. He'd also courteously declined the overtures of Confindustria, Italy's federation of employers.

I couldn't say why I'd chosen him as a strategic cornerstone for my creative criminality. On the one hand I was pretty certain that someone who steers such a careful path must be no better than all the rest, only smarter, because you just don't rise to certain levels unless you're a real son of a bitch. In the best sense of the term, of course. Moreover, he did everything possible to stand out from the crowd, he was painstakingly stylish, and he refused to go along with the standard procedures of his milieu: these things made me feel close to him and even similar to him. I felt sure we'd get along.

Roby De Palma was a man of his word and he secured a meeting for me with a guy in his early sixties, with a creased face and the callused hands of a lifetime of hard manual labor.

"I was told to come talk to you," he said without preamble, in dialect.

I handed him the CD I'd burned with the audio recording of Ylenia's voice as she dug a shallow grave for her lover. Just a few choice extracts, enough to give an idea of the quality of the merchandise.

"If he's interested, he knows how to get in touch with me."

But I couldn't manage to get in touch with Nicoletta. I doubted that she had fallen into the Palamaras' hands. They'd have already withdrawn their siege of La Nena and I'd already be dead, after a long and painful session in which I'd have given up all my secrets.

She was holed up somewhere, trying to live on her savings and make the best of life as it is. She'd never been the same after Isabel's death. Once again I found myself wishing that wherever she was holed up, it was someplace deep and distant. Outside of the country, ideally. Nicoletta wasn't the type to go to a monastery; she'd be more likely to head for a resort, where she could scrub her conscience clean with saunas and massages and vigorous sex with the local beefcakes.

"Giorgio, wake up."

I opened my eyes and looked up at the time projected on the ceiling by my clock radio. "It's 6 A.M. What the fuck were you thinking?"

"There's a guy who's come to pick you up," Martina explained. "Are you doing renovations or something at the restaurant?"

"Why do you ask?"

"He looks like a workman, I don't know, a plumber, maybe . . . "

I leapt to my feet. Now I knew who was waiting for me. I shuffled to the front door in my slippers, where the powerful man's emissary stood patiently, with his canvas painter's cap bearing the logo of a major brand of cattle feed in his hand.

"I'll be there in ten minutes."

I didn't have as much time as I would have liked to prepare for such an important meeting, but the surprise scheduling was certainly intentional. When I got into the man's compact car I tapped my jacket pocket one last time to make sure that I had brought the flash stick with Ylenia's interview.

I suffered with unruffled resignation through a wordless and lengthy drive, at low cruising speed, to an enormous country estate southwest of Ferrara. The car turned in through a wrought-iron gate and followed a drive leading to an old villa undergoing renovation. There was scaffolding everywhere as well as neat stacks of terracotta bricks and roof tiles. But there were no workers that day. Next to the entrance was a car I'd only seen in photographs. A Maybach 62S—half a million euros' worth of luxury automobile. A detail that made a good impression on me. A truly refined vehicle isn't common in the Veneto. Most of the rich people here like them flashy and loud.

An elegant woman of about fifty materialized at the door as if by enchantment. Her slender body was sheathed in a severe black tailored suit; her gray hair was pulled into an evanescent bun.

She smiled as she greeted me with exquisite courtesy, then she asked me to follow her. We walked through a succession of bare, dusty rooms until we reached a gleaming oak door. Considering the effort that the woman clearly expended in opening it, that door concealed a bulletproof armored core. I walked into a large office furnished in ultramodern style, with furniture unlike anything I'd ever seen, in sharp contrast with the collection of icons hanging on the wall.

I was stopped by a young man with "ex-cop" stamped on his face. He did a quick and professional body search.

"Forgive me for taking these precautions, Pellegrini," said the man who had agreed to meet with me. "You are a former terrorist, after all, and I've been in the crosshairs of your comrades in the Veneto for many years now."

"But it's been so long," I objected under my breath.

The bodyguard left the room and we were alone. I sat down on an uncomfortable yellow plastic chair.

"Pardon me if I have nothing to offer you, but this isn't my house. It belongs to a company and I'm just borrowing it for a couple of hours."

The message was unmistakable: this meeting never happened, and it would be impossible to prove otherwise.

He knit the fingers of his white, well-manicured hands together. "I listened to the material that you sent me and I want to start by telling you that I'm not interested in buying it or putting it on the market."

"Then why the fuck did you have someone come to my house and wake me up at six in the morning?" I thought before replying, more judiciously: "But I don't want to sell it."

"Then I'm afraid I don't quite understand."

I pulled out the flash stick and laid it on the table. "The material, as you call it, is actually a video and it's much longer, much more articulated, and infinitely more interesting. I just want to make it available to you."

"Explain what you mean."

"As you must have realized, the information concerns the Honorable Brianese and his vast network of clientelism and personal interests. Unfortunately, he's gone completely out of control and I've been a victim of his dirty dealings."

I told him about the fake investment in Dubai and the arrival of the Calabrians in response to my efforts to get back my two million euros. I told him about Tortorelli, his disappearance, and the way the Palamaras had been persecuting me.

He reached out, picked up the flash stick, and inserted it in the USB port of his PC. A few seconds later, Ylenia's voice emerged from the speakers.

"These statements were extorted under torture," he noted with some disappointment.

"I kind of lost my head," I admitted. "In any case, every word of Signorina Mazzonetto's statement is pure gold."

He watched the video from start to finish without moving a muscle. He pulled out the flash stick and gave it back to me. "You see, Signor Pellegrini, the very foundation of the Veneto rests on a clearly defined bloc of power, made up of the various manufacturers' associations, the Padanos, the party in which Brianese is so active, and responsible sectors of the trade unions. None of them really likes any of the others, but what cements the alliance into place is the fact that they each need the others. Do you follow me?"

I nodded, but the truth was I didn't have the slightest idea of what all that political folderol had to do with my money and the Palamaras.

"The situation in this country is fluid, but there will never be any real change in the Veneto, for the simple reason that no one is capable of modifying reality itself. There won't be any dramatic scandals like the ones that blight our unfortunate Italy, nor will there be any sweeping judicial investigations. Of any kind. We'll soon see a series of adjustments in the equilibrium between the Padanos and their allies due to internal issues that are going to result in a schism in the Northern Italian political front. These issues are going to be exacerbated by a number of minor judicial investigations that will single out regional officers suspected of financial crimes."

"I'm confused," I interrupted with a sense of unease. "I'm not sure what you're driving at."

"I was simply explaining to you why Brianese is untouchable and irreplaceable. I can also tell you confidentially that he's going to be appointed a cabinet minister."

"But I have no intention of trying to hurt him," I retorted.

"Then you misspoke a few minutes ago when you referred to the Honorable Brianese's 'dirty dealings,' am I right?"

I changed course instantly. "I only want him to go back to frequenting my establishment. La Nena will be at his complete disposal for all future election campaigns, but I'm not willing to be murdered just to get him off the hook, nor am I willing to let him steal my money."

"That's quite understandable."

I picked up the flash stick. "Well, do you want this or not?"

"If you insist in your determination to put it into my hands, courtesy demands at the very least that I accept it," he explained. "What use I may choose to make of it is none of your business."

He went back to his computer and I sat there like an idiot. I stood up, mumbled a farewell, and left the room. The woman with her hair in a bun walked me back to the car as if I were the King of Spain.

After a while, that long wordless return journey got on my nerves. "Is he always such an asshole?" I blurted out.

The driver laughed heartily. "His father was worse," he confided in dialect.

I was so furious and humiliated that I stayed away from the restaurant and from Martina and Gemma as well. I knew I was in a dangerous mood. I got in my car and drove aimlessly from one province to another, through an infinite network of bypasses, highways, bridges, and overpasses. Every so often I stopped to look at the landscape or the traffic. I'd finished high school and a few years of college. I'd grown up in an educated family. In other words, I wasn't a certified asshole but that's what I felt like. I couldn't decipher the meaning of the messages that the man I so admired had tossed offhandedly in my direction. All I knew was that right then and there, I felt like kicking him in the ass.

My cell phone rang. Caller unavailable. "It's Nicoletta. I heard you wanted to talk to me."

"Yeah. There are some people looking for you. You've absolutely got to disappear."

"Should I be afraid?"

"Very afraid. If they catch you they'll kill you."

"I'm not ready to leave. I need a few more days to wrap up some things."

"Then you're going to have to worry about me catching you before they do, because I can't run the risk of having you talk."

That scared her. "I have a friend who lives in New Zealand. I'll get a flight tomorrow."

"Get back in touch in six months and I'll let you know if it's safe to come back."

Had I made the right decision by letting her live? It certainly hadn't been prudent, but the conditions for her survival had been established by the intrinsic dynamics of criminal creativity. Attending her funeral was the last thing I could afford to do right now. And I really couldn't go out and dig another shallow grave in the little graveyard I'd created on Brianese's estate.

At the end of a dull day Ylenia showed up with a shopping bag made of organic cotton, filled with cash. "Fifty thousand euros a month till the debt is paid off."

"Has something happened that I don't know about?"

"It was Sante's decision," she replied. "I'd also like to ask you to be so kind as to come up with a menu and an estimate for a bridal shower."

"Who's the lucky girl?"

"I am."

"Who's the guy?"

"His name is Franco, you don't know him."

"And how did you meet him?"

She told me where he worked and everything became clear. "Another one of Sante's decisions, I assume?"

"For my own good," she lied to both of us.

I couldn't understand why the powerful man to whom I'd entrusted the Counselor's secrets should have decided to unite Ylenia in holy matrimony with his assistant, but it certainly did nothing to harm me. In fact, that first bag of fifty thousand euros was a clear sign that Brianese had been forcefully advised to reconsider my legitimate requests.

I looked at the two Calabrians who were stuffing their faces with hors d'oeuvres and prosecco at my expense. There was no way of getting rid of them.

I'd have to wait a few more months. Then, finally, one night I feasted my eyes on the television screen and the sight of the Palamaras in handcuffs, being carted off to prison. Giuseppe glared into the TV camera with fierce contempt.

One of the investigating judges clearly spoke about dealings between the 'Ndrangheta and politicians in Lombardy. One of the men who were arrested was identified as a major vote bundler.

If I wanted proof that the Calabrians would stop persecuting me, the clincher came later that day: they didn't show up in the restaurant. I couldn't be sure that Giuseppe would forget about yours truly and the humiliation I'd inflicted on him with my creative criminality, but he had other things to think about for the moment.

At the end of a dull day La Nena was packed with beautiful people celebrating Sante Brianese's appointment as cabinet minister. The powerful man had predicted everything down to the smallest details. The Padanos had proven incapable of exploiting their victory and they had some serious internal fleas to scratch. The Counselor was a rising star but the prestigious government appointment would force him to abandon the Veneto once and for all and someone else would have to take over his network of dealings. Politics too was a form of creative criminality. In fact, it was creative criminality taken to its logical extreme. I might be excluded from the field of political endeavor entirely, but I'd decided to stay right where I was. I was born to ass-fuck my fellow man and it was something I really enjoyed. It made me feel alive. I had the distinct sensation that I had absorbed the life force of all the people I'd eliminated from the face of the earth, but maybe that was just the euphoria of victory, or at least of knowing that I'd come home alive but still having a hard time believing it. Now I'd need to look around and build new alliances, connections, and connivances. I'd have to grow a new politician all my own. Let him use La Nena as a springboard and then tend to him throughout the course of his career: city government, provincial government, regional government. I wasn't looking for a rising star, like Brianese ten years ago. I needed a competent midfielder.

Signora Ombretta Brianese née Marenzi moved away from her husband's side and came over to me. She gave me a sly, knowing glance and kept taking small sips of bubbly. The ring of lipstick on the champagne glass looked like a spot of fresh blood and she looked like a beautiful vampiress who had just banqueted.

She tossed back the flute of champagne at a single gulp and then handed it to me as if I were a waiter. Not a particularly attractive gesture for a lady of her class. "That villa in the countryside outside of Ferrara has belonged to my family for three generations," she revealed with ill concealed pleasure, confident that the news would take me by surprise. "And I've been a close friend of the gentleman that you met since I was a child."

"So Ylenia's wedding was your idea."

"Let's just say that I wanted to make sure that a deeply unhappy future lay in wait for her."

I shifted my gaze over to Brianese. "But that means your husband loses out, too."

She snorted. "He may have lots of good qualities, but he's still just an insatiable parvenu. He'll cause less damage in Rome."

"In the end, you're always the ones who clean things up and make them presentable, aren't you?"

"Who are you referring to, Signor Pellegrini?"

"The powerful families. The families that matter. The families that have always called the shots. Which is exactly why I got in touch with your old childhood friend from happy days gone by," I replied irreverently.

Ombretta avoided responding and turned her back on me to graciously accept a compliment from the chief of the city police.

Rivers of champagne were flowing and for once I wasn't giving out so much as a free toothpick. Midway through the evening I found a free corner of the bar and enjoyed a glass in blessed peace. Brianese was emanating happiness from every pore, Ylenia had her arms wrapped around her new true love, and Martina and Gemma were chatting with friends and acquaintances.

I had big plans for the two women. A daily routine involving a wife and a lover would degenerate into pure absurdity. But the three of us living together would be a perfect solution. That very night I was planning to tell my wife that as a woman she wasn't complete because she lacked a live-in girlfriend with whom she could have sex on a regular basis. I would ladle a countercultural sauce of Sixties-style pearls of wisdom over the whole thing. "Free Love." "Unleash the love that's sleeping inside you," I'd whisper into her ear while caressing her thighs. The idea might frighten her at first, then she'd accept the new situation and place it within the complexity of a love as grand as ours.

It wouldn't take the same amount of chitchat with Gemma. The King of Hearts would give an order and she would obey with wholehearted enthusiasm. I'd develop a schedule of activities designed to keep both of them in shape, but first of all we'd have a plastic surgeon do a series of minor tweaks to our little girlfriend.

I greeted an art dealer who was helping me procure a painting by my beloved Grace Slick. I pointed to the wall I'd chosen, and she took a picture with her cell phone so she could select the frame. Then she went back to mingling with the other guests.

When I'd first shown her the painting on the Internet she'd made some comment about it being just a little too "flower power" to fit in with the interior decoration of La Nena.

"That's me, in the middle, in the hat, running across the field," I retorted, pointing out a detail.

She went on blathering some nonsense about the intrinsic metamessage contained in the act of purchasing the painting, then she asked me how I intended to pay. When I flashed her a wad of cash, her face lit up and she forgave my supposed lapse in taste.

The painting by my beloved Grace, hanging strategically across from the cash register, would help me to inject a stimulating and fecund dose of imagination into the vein of creative criminality, a pursuit to which I intended to devote myself regularly from now on.

I would no longer get bogged down in activities like the prostitution ring, which demanded a special dedicated logistical structure and organization. Flexibility would be the order of the creative local economy. Applied to my personal sector, it translated into a regular practice of robbing large amounts of money that had been procured through corruption. If restricted to that sector, armed robbery would immediately become a much less risky way of doing business. It meant the elimination of police reports and accompanying investigations.

An elegantly dressed gentleman who was new to the city was mingling with the guests. He was the head of a holding company that defrauded companies undergoing bankruptcy proceedings. Ylenia had explained to me how, in exchange for fifteen percent of the debt paid in crisp new bills, the man pretended to purchase the companies with the promise that he'd turn them around. Instead he'd transfer ownership to foreign corporations, pocket the money, and abandon the entrepreneurs to their fate. He explained to the suckers that the mechanism that would save them from their creditors, the banks, and the tax department was a judicial safeguard consisting of the term: "letter of indemnity."

A lightning hunch had led me to cut that information from the interview with Brianese's secretary, and I was glad I had done so, since the asshole in question was cruising my restaurant in search of victims.

All he had to do was snooker one of my customers and word would get out that you had to watch your step at La Nena. That wasn't going to happen, however. I'd clean the guy out and then send him to prison. Not because I had any problem with the idea of shooting him dead, but because there were too many people involved, and I couldn't hope to kill them all. I'd be very pleased to give credit for removing them from circulation to the Carabinieri. The plan was still a nebulous cloud of images and thoughts. Inspiration would certainly come with the information that I was gathering.

I caught the man's eye and raised my glass in his direction. Then I came out from behind the counter and walked toward him, with a great show of deference.

"There's nothing better than a flute of champagne to set things right at the end of a dull day," I said as I extended a glass to him.

"Are you the proprietor?"

"Yes, La Nena is my private kingdom and I'm Giorgio Pellegrini."

About the Author

Massimo Carlotto is one of the best-known living crime writers in Europe. In addition to the many titles in his extremely popular "Alligator" series, and his stand-alone noir novels, he is also the author of *The Fugitive*, in which he tells the story of his arrest and trial for a crime he didn't commit, and his subsequent years on the run. Carlotto's novel *The Goodbye Kiss* was a finalist for the MWA's Edgar Award for Best Novel.

"You *are* embarrassing me," he accuses triumphantly. "You're being sarcastic."

"Big shot!" I tell him sarcastically. "You don't even know what embarrass means."

"Yes, I do. And I know what sarcastic means. It means when you're doing something I don't want you to do."

"I'm not doing anything you don't want me to do. I'm not doing anything at all but standing here, so how can I be embarrassing you?"

"You're asking me questions, aren't you? Why do you keep asking me questions?"

"Why don't you answer them?"

"I'm going to tell Mommy," he threatens. "I'm going to tell Mommy you drank whiskey."

"She won't believe you. She'll know it's a lie."

"How come?"

"Your nose will grow."

"How come?"

"A person's nose grows when he tells a lie."

"Then *your* nose is growing," he counters. "Because *that's* a lie."

"Then why would my nose be growing if it's a lie?"

"I'm going to sock you one, Daddy," he squeals in frustration, as he feels himself outsmarted.

"Why are you twisting around so much? Stand still."

"I think I'm nervous," he guesses.

"Do you have to pee? Then why are you picking at your pecker?"

"I don't like that."

(He stops picking at his pecker. I'm sorry I said it.)

"She'll smell my breath," I resume, to change *that* subject. "She won't smell whiskey, and that's how she'll know you're lying."

"I'm going to kick you," he says. "I think I'm going to kick you in the shins."

"Why?" I ask in surprise.

"Because," he says. "Because whenever I kick you in the

shins or sock you c
laugh a lot, so I thin.

"I'll kick your as

"I'm going to te

"So what? I say

"She doesn't like

"We don't fight."

"You fight a lot. S

"She doesn't smac

"She cries."

"No, she doesn't."

"Sometimes she do

"You talk too muc
you get them all mixed u

"I wish I knew some
me, kidding.

"Why?"

"I'm going to call a c

"Why?"

"To smack you."

"He's not allowed to."

"You smack me."

"I'm allowed to. And I

"You used to."

"I did not. In your wh
once."

"Once you did. When I v

"If I did, I'm sorry. But
you now. Do I?"

"You're going to. Aren't y

"For what?"

"You know."

"I'm not."

"You promise?"

"I promise."

"You promise you won't sm

"I promise."

"You really

"I promise

"I believe

And *wham*

I leap a n
know I must lo
in outrage, str
laugh immedi
he has perha
sees and hear
hurt nor disp
sunburst of
exaggerate al
laughing and
doubled over
gulping and
him: I hurl
we fall to the
the beginnin
ing for air
until I grow
me. I am out
he isn't sati
savor his v
experiment
toeholds. M
(another le
one should
thing abou
is that soo
my boy is f
foot, not c
my muscle
one brief
around d
excitemen
and elbo

animal trying energetically to fight and wiggle free as I swarm down upon him. (Now I cannot let him win; if I do, he'll know it's only because I did let him, and then he'll know that he has lost.) It is no contest at all now that I have my wind back and am going about it in earnest. I employ my greater bulk (much of it solid flab, ha, ha) to force him down into place. It is relatively easy for me to grasp both his wrists in one of my hands, to immobilize his legs beneath the pressing weight of my own and end his kicking. In just a few more seconds it is over; and he gives up. I have him nailed to the ground in a regulation pin. We stare at each other smiling, our faces inches apart.

"I win," he jokes.

"Then let me up," I joke back.

"Only if you surrender," he says.

"I surrender," I reply.

"Then I'll let you up," he says.

I let him go and we rise slowly, breathing hard and feeling close to each other.

"You know, Daddy," he starts right in with pious gravity, trying to divert me, assuming an owlish and censorious expression as austerely as a judge, "I really did win, because you threw sand in my eyes and tickled me and that's not allowed."

"I did not," I retort fliply.

"Did you tickle me? You liar."

"That's allowed. You can tickle."

"You don't laugh."

"You don't know how to tickle."

"That's why it's not fair."

"It is fair. And furthermore," I continue, "I didn't throw sand."

"I can say you did."

"And did you know, by the way, that it's a lovely day today because the sun is shining and the bay is calm and blue, and there are nine or seven planets—"

"Nine."

"—of which Mercury is closest to the sun and . . ."

"Pluto."

". . . Pluto is the farthest?"

"Did you hear about the homosexual astronauts?" he asks.

"Yes. They went to Uranus. And if, as they say, there are seven days in each week and fifty-two weeks in each year, how come there are three hundred and sixty-five days in the year instead of three hundred and sixty-four?"

He pauses to calculate. "How come?" he queries. "I never thought about that."

"I don't know. I never thought about it either."

"Is that what you want to talk about now?" he asks disconsolately.

"No. But if you want to stall, I'll stall along with you. You're not fooling me."

"I'm going to tell Mommy," he threatens again. "I'm going to tell Mommy you threw sand in my eyes."

"*I'm* going to tell her," I rejoin.

"Are you?" His manner turns solemn.

"What?"

"Going to tell her?"

"What?"

"You know."

"What?"

"What I did?"

"Did you do something?" I inquire with airy candor.

"You know."

"I can't remember."

"What I gave away."

"Did you give something away?"

"Daddy, you know I gave a nickel away."

"When? You give a lot of nickels away."

"Just before. When you were right here."

"Why?"

"You won't know."

"Tell me why. How do you know?"

"You'll get angry and start yelling or begin to tease me or make fun of me."

"I won't. I promise."

"I wanted to," he states simply.

"That's no answer."

"I knew you'd say that."

"I knew you'd say that."

"I said you wouldn't understand."

"He didn't ask you for it," I argue. "He couldn't believe his eyes when you gave it to him. I don't think you even know him that long. I'll bet you don't even like him that much. Do you?"

"You're getting angry," he sulks. "I knew you would."

"I'm not."

"You're starting to yell, aren't you?"

"I'm just raising my voice."

"You see?"

"You're faking," I charge, and give him a tickling poke in the ribs. "And I know you're faking, so stop faking and trying to pretend you can fool me. Answer."

He grins sheepishly, exposed and pleased. "I don't know. I don't know if I like him or not. I only met him yesterday."

"See? I'm smart. Then why? You know what I mean. Why did you give your money to him?"

"You'll think I'm crazy."

"Maybe you are."

"Then I won't tell you."

"I know you aren't."

"Do I have to?"

"Yes. No. You want to. I can see you do. So you have to. Come on."

"I wanted to give him something," he explains very softly. "And that was all I had."

"Why did you want to give him something?"

"I don't know."

He tells me this so plainly, truthfully, innocently as to

make it seem the most plausible and obvious reason imaginable. And I do understand. His frankness is touching, and I feel like reaching out to embrace him right there on the spot and rewarding him with dollar bills. I want to kiss him (but I think he will be embarrassed if I do, because we are out in public). I want to tousle his hair lightly. (I do.) Tenderly, I say to him:

"That's still no answer."

"How come?" he inquires with interest.

"It doesn't tell why."

"It's why."

"It doesn't tell why you wanted to give him something. Why did you want to give him something?"

"I think I know. You sure keep after me, don't you?"

"Why did you want to give him something?"

"Do I have to tell?"

"No. Not if you don't want to."

"I was happy," he states with a shrug, squinting uncomfortably in the sunlight, looking a little pained and self-conscious.

"Yeah?"

"And whenever I feel happy," he continues, "I like to give something away. Is that all right?"

"Sure." (I feel again that I want to kiss him.)

"It's okay?" He can hardly trust his good fortune.

"And I'm glad you were happy. Why were you happy?"

"Now it gets a little crazy."

"Go ahead. You're not crazy."

"Because I knew I was going to give it away." He pauses a moment to giggle nervously. "To tease you," he admits. "Then when I knew I was happy about that, I wanted to give the nickel away because I was happy about wanting to give the nickel away. Is it okay?"

"You're making me laugh."

"You're not mad?"

"Can't you see that you're making me laugh? How can I be mad?"